A Rake by Reputation

Westham Chronicles, Volume 1

Meg Osborne

Published by Meg Osborne, 2023.

A RAKE BY REPUTATION

First edition. January 6, 2023.

Copyright © 2023 Meg Osborne.

ISBN: 979-8215335666

Written by Meg Osborne.

Chapter One

Sir Benjamin Devereaux discovered he was a *sir* on a Tuesday. Up until then, he had been plain old Benjamin or *Mr Devereaux* from those trying to promote an acquaintance, and there were not a great many of *those*, for, along with his good looks and charm, Benjamin Devereaux was in possession of one thing most young men of eight-and-twenty sought to avoid: a reputation.

"Come on, Devereaux!" George Lennox moaned, folding his tall, well-built figure into a chair clearly not designed for such wanton lounging. "Put your papers down for the day and come out with me. Surely you must be finished by now!"

"Almost." Ben's voice was little more than a whisper and he cleared his throat, scanning the letter he held once more before laying it down with a short, bitter laugh. This caught his friend's ear and at once Lennox sat up straighter.

"Do share the joke, Dev," he urged, folding his arms politely and turning what he evidently thought was a curious gaze upon his friend. "Enquiring minds would like to know what it is that can make the perpetually ill-tempered Benjamin Devereaux laugh."

"That's *Sir Benjamin* to you, Lennox," Ben said, tapping one finger on the letter. "As of a few days ago."

Lennox frowned as if he were not quite sure whether his friend spoke the truth or was laying a linguistic trap.

"It's very simple, old man." Ben leaned back in his seat, regarding his friend across the wide expanse of his heavy oak desk. "Sadly, it appears my father has met with an illness he could not bellow into submission. As his eldest and only son, his title passes directly to me." His smile grew cynical and sly. "Along with the estate in the country, and this fine establishment. Within which, you have been making yourself quite at home this past year."

"Heavens, Dev." George's face had paled. He had the grace to look a little sober for the first time in their acquaintance. Devereaux knew he ought to explain quite quickly that there was very little love lost between the young Ben and his lately departed father. He rather liked seeing the usually light-hearted George Lennox rendered serious for once. "I'm sorry for -"

"Do not mention *my loss*," Ben muttered, his voice dangerously low. "That man may have been my father, but his departure from this earth is no loss to me. We last spoke a decade ago, and I have managed perfectly well for the past ten years without him. I dare say I shall continue to survive in his absence." He tried to smile, but the expression felt strange and forced. Clearing his throat, he tried again. "I wonder if I can avail myself of a visit to the country as soon as this week. I should like to see the old place again..."

His eyes closed as he conjured the dappled sunlight and greenery of his childhood. He was just reconstructing the walled garden that had been his mother's domain when the memory shifted. It was not his mother's light, musical voice he recalled but another woman's harsh cry. His eyes flew open and he saw his hands tightening around the edge of the desk with such force his knuckles had turned white.

"Well, now you *must* come and have a drink with me," Lennox declared, watching his friend carefully. "To celebrate your father's life and mourn his passing." His expression shifted into a dark smile. "Or to mourn his life and celebrate his passing, I leave the choice to you. Either way, there ought to be brandy. As but one of us is now endowed with a title, I shall allow your purse-strings to stretch on this occasion. Let's go to the club and see if any of the others are about."

Devereaux cracked a smile, feeling the tension ebb from his limbs. George Lennox was able to wring an excuse for drinking out of anything but in this case, perhaps he was right. Ben didn't need to make any decisions right away. His eyes narrowed dangerously. Silence would be a weapon in its own right. No doubt his stepmother would be worried enough about what the new Sir Benjamin's first actions might be. Why not let her stew a little longer?

"Very well, Lennox. You have been a very patient companion while I attended to my papers. Come along. I suppose I ought to make the most of being here while I still can before my new responsibilities call me away."

"Indeed!" Lennox beamed and launched himself towards the door.

Ben folded his letter neatly, with care that bordered on reverence. He slid it into a pocket, feeling the absurd notion that he needed to keep it close, a talisman against too much merriment - or too much melancholy, he was not quite sure to which he was most inclined at present. A reminder of where he had come from and, now, who he had become...

Sir Benjamin Devereaux. He turned the name over in his mind, wondering how long it would be before it lost all association with his distant, difficult father and became entirely his own.

ROLAND PARK WAS SO familiar to Amelia Sudbury that she had tripped quite comfortably over the threshold that morning with a basket for her friend and been a little surprised to find the great house still shrouded in silence. A servant with drawn features, perpetually shooting a glance overhead, ushered her into the spacious parlour, where, to Amelia's relief, she could see her friend, Joanna Devereaux, already waiting for her.

"I came to see you," Amelia said, shedding her cloak and hurrying close enough to embrace her friend. "I ought not to have left it so long, but Papa -" She went white, and swallowed the rest of her words. *How cruel!* To mention one's own father in the presence of the friend who had recently lost hers.

"I am sorry, Joanna," she blurted, wishing that she was better able to control her wretched tongue, which was forever getting her into one scrape or another.

"Sorry?" Joanna smiled, sadly. "Why should you be sorry? None of this is your fault, and I am very glad you have come to see us." Her expression was pained. "Or, come to see me, at least. I am afraid Mama is not able to take visitors at present, nor will she be for some time yet, I fear."

Amelia nodded. What grief the poor Lady Devereaux must still be feeling at the loss of her husband!

"You mustn't mind Mama," Joanna continued, urging her friend closer to the fire. "It's just that it all came as such a shock."

This was enough to make Amelia's eyebrows lift, despite her best attempts at remaining composed. *A shock?* Sir Benjamin had been unwell for almost as long as Amelia had known him. The old man was an invalid and Amelia recalled only too well being told off for her high spirits as she and her young friend had frolicked around the grand estate of Roland Park.

"I am very sorry for her," Amelia said, reaching across and taking hold of Joanna's hand warmly. "But it is you that I am most concerned for. My dear friend, I wish there was something I could do to help you bear your loss."

"You do help me, by being here!" Joanna exclaimed, smiling at Amelia and looking, for a moment, almost like her old, mischievous self. "I do not know how I should bear *Mama's* grief, let alone my own, without company."

As if on cue, there was a loud wail from overhead, and Joanna shuddered.

"How long - how long has she been confined to her room?" Amelia asked, wanting, and yet not wanting, to enquire after her friend's mother. She had never been particularly fond of Lady Devereaux, who had always acted as if she were a little above Amelia's own family and tolerated her presence at the house only as a friend for Joanna when there was nobody better. There had been talk of London, and Amelia had braced herself for the loss of her closest friend, but before Lady

Devereaux could have her way, her husband had died and the household had been thrown into chaos.

"Oh, a week at least!" Joanna said.

Amelia nodded, slowly, her mind turning this detail over. A week? Why, Sir Benjamin had been dead a fortnight! How was it that Lady Devereaux had not been overtaken immediately with her grief?

"It is not for Papa she cries," Joanna murmured as if reading her friend's mind. She kept her eyes fixed on the fire as if, by not looking at Amelia as she spoke, she could not be accused of betraying her mother's confidence. "She would like us to think that it is, that she grieves and mourns the loss of her husband, but in truth, all this weeping and wailing began upon the receipt of a certain letter."

A letter! This was intriguing indeed. Amelia slid her chair closer to her friend, leaning her elbows on her knees and watching Joanna carefully. She was piecing together her response but it seemed as if merely being there and allowing Joanna to speak as she chose, without clarification or interruption, was service enough. Joanna's eyes, bright with excitement, met Amelia's. Her cheeks were pink, either from nerves or their proximity to the fire, Amelia could not tell.

"She does not know that I saw it, of course, for almost as soon as it had been read she tore it into strips and cast it into the fire."

Joanna reached for the poker and jabbed at the embers as if recalling the action she had taken on this particular afternoon.

"Mama did not notice that a large fragment fell down into the grate, singed, but not destroyed." Biting her lip, she reached beneath a cushion and retrieved the offending fragment. "Here, Amelia. Read it, do, and tell me your thoughts."

Amelia's heart beat fast but she did as her friend instructed, unfolding a scrap of paper carefully, for fear of doing still more damage to it, and smoothing it carefully on her skirt.

"*...my dear lady, no, I will not call you...*
...return soon to claim my inheritance, but...
...will endeavour to show you the same grace...
...expect me then. I shall remain...

"Why, this could mean anything!" Amelia laughed or tried to, but the sound was strangled, and, rather than having the effect she had intended, which had been to soothe her friend's worries, this served only to inflame them.

"Oh, but it does not! Amelia, I know precisely what it means. Do you not recognise his hand?"

Amelia applied her eyes once more to the fragment, but she could not see whatever it was that seemed so apparent to her friend. The handwriting was elegant, suggesting that whoever had penned the letter was educated and erudite, but that could account for almost anybody in the departed Sir Benjamin's acquaintance. Surely nobody of that class would be cause enough for his widow to take to her bed in hysterics for seven days straight?

With a patient sigh, Joanna reached for the note, folding it carefully and slipping it back out of sight. She smiled, grimly.

"It is my brother, Amelia. Ben - well, now, I suppose we must call him Sir Benjamin, for the title has passed to him." She looked around her. A fat tear rolled down one thin cheek. "As does this house. Oh, Amelia! He means to come here and evict us. That is why Mama wails so. Not because of Papa, but because - because - we are about to be left destitute and homeless!"

Chapter Two

"**D**estitute and homeless! Those are the very words she used, Papa. Can you imagine such a tyrant as the new Sir Benjamin, to eject his own mother and sister out onto the street?"

Admiral Sudbury harrumphed, muttering something unintelligible from behind his newspaper.

Amelia ceased her pacing and settled into her own chair at her father's right-hand-side, peering over the top of his newspaper to meet a pair of misty grey eyes that looked very much like her own, albeit surrounded by a few more wrinkles and far bushier grey eyebrows.

"*Stepmother*," Admiral Sudbury remarked, for the second time. With a flourish, he folded

his newspaper and set it down on the side-table, before regarding his daughter carefully. "She is Devereaux's stepmother. And Joanna is his half-sister."

"What difference does that make?" Amelia exclaimed, throwing her hands up in despair and leaping to her feet once more. "They are family nonetheless, and he could not be so wicked as to banish them from their own home."

Admiral Sudbury's eyes twinkled.

"I would imagine a young lady who reads as many novels as you do has rather more grasp than that on the ability of villains to be wicked." He chuckled. "Assuming, of course, your Sir Benjamin Devereaux is a villain."

"I fail to see how he could not be considered so!" Amelia cried. "And do not refer to him as *my* anybody, Papa, for you know I have never so much as laid eyes on the man."

"And yet you profess to anticipate his every move before he has even set foot in Westham. Have you taken to divination in your spare time? Ought I to summon the curate?"

"Papa!" Amelia huffed. "I do not know why I attempt to converse with you about such things. You are wilfully obtuse and exist only to plague me."

"Whereas you exist only to please me, little daughter, which you do." He patted the seat next to him. "Even when you refuse to sit still for more than minute. Come, Milly, and rest, for your constant toing and froing is enough to drive a man to distraction." He grimaced. "Or sea-sickness."

"Ha!" Amelia barked but sank obediently into her chair nonetheless. "If you intend to convince me that you, an admiral, might be driven to sea-sickness by a little pacing when you survived circumnavigating the globe twice and more than one infamous battle, I shall assure you, you will not succeed."

"And yet, you are still, so perhaps the victory is mine in the end." Her father elbowed her gently in the ribs. "Now, tell me the rest of your story. What makes poor Miss Devereaux so convinced that she and her mother are about to be displaced?"

"Well -" Amelia faltered. Surely her father would not approve of Joanna's discovering the truth by deceit and sleight of hand. He was a stickler for privacy and word that Lady Devereaux's correspondence had fallen into the wrong hands might be just the motivation he needed to march Amelia back over to Roland Park immediately and admit everything to the bedridden Lady. Amelia swallowed, busily conjuring some manner by which the girls might have made their discovery without betraying her friend's actions.

"He - he wrote to tell them of his imminent arrival," she said, at last, trusting that this would not demand any further explanation. "Although Joanna was given little information beyond that. She is fearful that he returns to claim the estate, along with his title, and force them out."

"And why do you think him capable of such -" He assumed a tremulous voice. "*Villainy*?"

Amelia frowned sternly at him.

"Why, Father. Surely you have heard even more than I have about Benjamin Devereaux's misdeeds?"

Admiral Sudbury's eyebrows lifted, but he said nothing and Amelia was forced to share the little she knew.

"Well, he is a dreadful r-reprobate." Amelia flinched, stopping herself at the last minute from uttering the dreaded "rake". It might be the sort of word she used with her friends, that Joanna herself had applied to her half-brother whenever his name was mentioned, with a silent shock at the recollection of his being sent away.

"A reprobate?" The admiral's eyes twinkled. "And how came you to know this, if you haven't actually met the man?"

"Well, people say -"

"What people?"

Her father's voice had taken on the barking, belligerent tone he normally reserved for the ladies of Westham whenever they had begun to annoy him with their speculation and conjecture. Admiral Sudbury disliked gossip more than any other sin, and at that moment Amelia felt as if her father's ire was only moments away from being turned towards her.

"I only know what Joanna told me, Father, and surely she must know if she is Devereaux's sister."

"Half-sister," the admiral reminded her. "And were you not the first to remind me that they had not laid eyes on one another in over a decade?" He cleared his throat, noisily, and retrieved the cast-off newspaper. "I dare say she had a great many terrifying tales to tell of her absent half-brother." He harrumphed. "I dare say one or two of them might even be true or have their roots in truth. But I do not think that means we ought to construct a fully-formed opinion of a man we have yet to meet. Would you like the same to be done of you?"

Amelia flinched, knowing that this was uttered without malice, but with concern. Admiral Sudbury, himself, had been on the receiving end of cruel tongues wagging. Indeed, there had been enough gossip about his past, enough complaint about the ability of penniless sailors to raise themselves to esteem that it had cost him more than one romance in his youth.

It had taken him a long time to meet and marry Amelia's mother, he often remarked, so that when she died he could not even begin to contemplate marrying again. When Amelia's brother had followed their father into the navy, he uprooted their small family to Westham and settled into a life of near seclusion. Amelia would want for nothing except company. Westham was little more than a hamlet, and everybody knew one another's business. Amelia, fond of books, longed for a little adventure to come her way, just once.

"Perhaps you are right, Father," she said, eager to placate him. She dropped a penitent kiss on his balding head. "I ought not to judge Sir Benjamin Devereaux before I know him. But I certainly shan't warm to him if his coming means my only friend is sent away!"

⚜

DEVEREAUX HAD A HEADACHE and not one that was the unfortunate result of too much merriment the previous evening. It was little to boast of at present, mired as he was in the business of packing up his London life and returning home. Along with his father's land and title, he seemed to have inherited his debts, a mountain of paperwork that arrived on his desk in dribs and drabs, or handed to him by any one of several nameless, grey-featured fellows who referred to themselves, with great pride as *Sir Benjamin's solicitor.*

If they are all to be believed, my father possessed a solicitor for every day of the week, Ben thought, with a grimace. *And two for Sundays!*

He had known his father's business interests were diverse, but he had not imagined them to be as poorly managed as they had been. His father seemed to cast off his caution when he did his son, leaving the estate suffering the results of a decade's mismanagement. It would have been a mess even without the exuberant spending habits of the current Lady Devereaux.

Ben's head pounded even more ferociously at the thought of his stepmother. He had written to her, once, in acknowledgement of the news of his father's passing. He had not wanted to. The word, after all, of Sir Benjamin's death had not come from her pen, but that of the local curate, who wrote sorrowfully to have missed the young Benjamin Devereaux's presence at the burial of the older. *I would have come,* he raged, internally, *had I known about it before the old man was buried under the earth!* This was another sin he would not easily forgive his stepmother, and he had told her as much in the first letter he wrote. That particular note ended up in the fire - the very fire that still blazed in the hearth before him. It had taken one letter for him to vent his feelings towards the woman who had ruined his relationship with his father and then, not counting herself satisfied with poisoning Ben's memory of the old man, had prevented him the opportunity to make a final farewell. Such a letter was so peppered with invective that, whilst therapeutic in the writing, it would do him no favours to have read. So, into the fire it had gone, and an altogether more measured response penned in its place.

My dear Lady, he had begun, treating her with the deference her position, if not her person, deserved. He outlined his plan to come to Westham at his next available opportunity to make arrangements for their future in person, *for it is ill-fitting to have these arrangements made by letter.* That had been a sly dig at the dismissal he had received, by letter, ten years ago. The note had advised him to make other arrangements for his lodgings in future, for Roland Park could no longer be home to him. He doubted such a blow would even register, and so had persisted in his original goal, to heap hot coals on his stepmother's head and keep his true feelings to himself. *I shall return soon to claim my inheritance, but you need not fear for yourself or for Josie, who I do not doubt is quite the young lady these days. I will endeavour to show you the same grace I wish had been shown to me in the past...* She would not believe this show of chivalry, Ben expected, for such a woman would be poised, always, to see in others the motives she herself operated under.

"Let her stew on it," he mused aloud, as he closed one last ledger. The idea of the great Lady Devereaux, huge and imposing in his memory, although she must, in truth, be nought but an ordinary woman, brought low in trying to decode the contents of a simple letter had brought him a measure of amusement while he sifted for sense in his father's accounts, and the headache receded to a dull ache.

Pushing his chair back from his solid oak desk, he stood, walking towards the window and peering out into the hustle and bustle of the London street. He would miss this. The busyness of the city, its energy. Much as he bemoaned it to his friends, he did not entirely object to life in London. He objected to the fact that he had no alternative. Had he been entirely free in his movements, he might have quite enjoyed the change of pace between London and the country, the country and London.

A slow smile crept onto his features, rendering him almost handsome in the pale reflection he could just about make out in the glass. Necessity would no longer keep him here, or in any place except for that which he chose. He was entirely free of all entanglements and might return home as often as he wished and stay as long as he wished. His stepmother no longer had any say over his movements, and he had no need to fear to upset her on his father's behalf.

Idly, he watched a child break into a run before being halted and scooped up, scolded and set down again by his guardian, and Ben felt his heart constrict, again, and then burst into life.

"Bates!" he barked, summoning his valet, who had appeared with an answering knock at the study door even before Dev turned around. "Pack up my things and have them sent on after me. I am in no mood to wait, but shall begin my journey this afternoon."

"Sir?" Bates seemed poised to question him, but one look at the determined set of Devereaux's face evidently caused him to think better of the impulse.

"My carriage is ready, I presume?"

"Well -" Bates swallowed any objection, nodding twice in quick succession. "I will instruct the stables to have it ready for use within the hour. And your belongings, such as are already packed, may go with you now, the rest to be sent on after you, sir."

"Excellent." Ben could not stop the smile growing on his face. A real smile, now, the first genuine one he had worn since the news had reached him of his father's death. He would not mourn the death directly, although he mourned what relationship they might have had, had either one of them been less proud, less set in their ways and more able to bridge the gap that had begun their estrangement. He lifted his chin. Certainly, he sought to become a better *Sir Benjamin* than his father had ever been, and the first step along that smooth path involved going back to Roland Park and seeing, for himself, the state of things. His course set, his decision made, he could not bear to linger any longer in London, however many friends he had nearby, and however many entertainments he knew of in close proximity to his house. He wanted to be in Westham again, to feel the breeze at his back and the grass beneath his feet.

Leaning over his desk, he scratched out a quick note for his friends outlining his plans and sealed it, passing it to Bates.

"See that Mr Lennox receives this, will you? Tell him, if he wishes to reach me in the foreseeable future that he must look for me at Roland Park." His smile dimmed, his voice growing serious. "It's time I was at home again."

Chapter Three

Amelia pulled her wrap closer, wishing she had taken her father up on his offer to drive her by carriage that afternoon. It was not a great distance to town and a walk that she had made so often alone or with friends that she knew it by heart. On that particular afternoon, there was a bitter wind that whipped around her shoulders, teasing her hair from beneath her bonnet, and making her breath freeze in her lungs.

It had been an entirely fruitless journey, too, for she had gone to find something new to read, to replace a hair-ribbon that had, at last, been given up for lost, and to deliver a letter. Not a single task had she accomplished, for the book-seller had had no new delivery and had remarked, rather caustically, that any young lady who so rigorously devoured novels as she did was at risk of coming to a bad end. The only hair-ribbons she could find were a particularly hideous shade of mustard that clashed horribly with her complexion. The letter she had managed to deliver, but not as she had planned because its recipient was not at home. She had left it for his attention but was a little disappointed, on her father's behalf, that there would be no immediate response. The admiral had few friends in Westham, being surrounded rather more than he wished to be by married couples and older widows. That they should benefit by the relatively recent arrival of a young gentleman curate had been something of a delight to her father. The two had developed a regular habit of playing chess, discussing politics and, when Admiral Sudbury's gout did not plague him too badly, of walking around the church grounds together. Alas, the admiral remained at home with his leg propped up, and the curate was nowhere to be found.

Frustrated with her day and the weather, Amelia lingered longer than she ought to have at the window of the dress-makers, imagining herself clad in beautiful blue silk, fitted with the new style of long sleeves just in time for the winter assembly that would take place in a few short weeks. Alas, there was no excuse for a new dress. Her father was a kind man and possessed a reasonable fortune amassed during his naval career. He was also thrifty and lacked the sensibilities of a woman when it came to expenditure on *frivolous non-necessities* such as dresses. On books, he might be a little more easily persuaded, for he wished to encourage his daughter to think as well as her brother did, and saw books as a means to do this, even if he despaired over Amelia's choices. She sighed and turned for home, thinking that at that moment she would not object to reading *The Italian* for the tenth time, if she could do it tucked up under a blanket, with a hot cup of tea to warm her icy fingers.

Deviating from the well-worn road, she decided to take the path that would lead her past Roland Park on her way home. She might call in and spend a few minutes with Joanna so her outing need not be entirely wasted. This thought cheered her, and she walked with purpose, wrapping her arms around herself to ward off the wind that seemed to grow stronger with every step. She blinked away the tears that sprang up in the face of such cold and tried to enjoy the bright sunshine illuminating the stark trees, still stubbornly clinging to a few of their leaves despite the plummeting temperatures.

She had an ulterior motive for visiting Roland Park, although she would never admit as much to her friend. She wanted to catch a glimpse of the infamous Benjamin Devereaux. Since her father had taken her to task over listening to gossip about Sir Benjamin, Amelia had not spoken to him or to anyone about Joanna's half-brother. She had thought back over the stories she had heard, totting up his sins in a page of her journal. This book was a treasured gift, containing a record of all of her private thoughts and experiences. It made for dull reading, for very little seemed to happen in Westham. The return of a rake, as all she had heard about Benjamin Devereaux painted him to be, was a glimmer of excitement and Amelia certainly did not intend on squandering it.

As she drew within sight of the grand estate her heartbeat fervently in her chest, though she merely picked her way along paths she had walked freely for as long as she could remember. Today she felt nervous merely being there as if she was trespassing in a place she did not quite belong. It seemed like the house itself was watching her, and she glanced up at it, half-expecting to see a dark figure looming in one window. There was no such figure, and Amelia laughed at her own fancy, thinking that perhaps the book-seller was right and too many books were destroying her rational mind. She was startled into silence, though, when a low, masculine voice reached her, pinning her in place with a question.

"Does something about my home strike you as amusing? I did not realise it served to provoke laughter from strangers. Who are you and what are you doing here?"

❦

SHE DID NOT LOOK LIKE a trespasser, this young woman. Still, the way she jumped back, staring at him in shock surprised even Devereaux.

"Well?" he growled, before rethinking his strategy. One caught more flies with honey than vinegar, after all. "Are you lost?" He settled his features into a vague, innocuous smile, the kind he had perfected in company with Lennox, and which the latter used almost daily to ensnare just such an innocent young lady as this one. The smile became a grimace, and he sacrificed it altogether. "I asked you a question. Do you mean to answer it or continue to ignore me?"

"I - I'm sorry, sir -" The young lady's voice grew in confidence as she spoke, and her posture relaxed a little. It was subtle, but even Ben was aware of the shift in the air that existed between them. She was not so frightened now. He braced himself for her answer, expecting some practised coquetry of the sort he had left behind him in London. *This is the game we play, is not it?* his eyes asked her, silently mocking the intricate rules of courtship that his friends seemed to excel in and that he found tedious in extreme. *Well, my lady, I shall be a gentleman in this instance and allow you to set the pace.*

"I was looking for Miss Devereaux," she said, with an imperious toss of her golden head. "The lady of the house." Her eyes narrowed. "You, I take it, are her brother."

Her tone, which had softened at the mention of *Miss Devereaux,* had turned icy again as she referred to him, and he found her insolence amusing. Most young ladies, when confronted with Mr Benjamin Devereaux, even before he had become *Sir* would not so openly dismiss him.

"This is my house, Madam," he said, rocking back on his heels and surveying her out of the corner of his eye. "I think, therefore, you might refer to Miss Devereaux as *my sister*." He dropped in a bow, which seemed to catch the young lady before him still more off-guard, as she staggered back a step. "Sir Benjamin Devereaux. And you are...?"

"Amelia," she blurted, before regaining her footing and her confidence with another shake of her pretty brown curls. "Miss Amelia Sudbury."

He nodded, slowly, filing this piece of information away for when it might become useful in future. He tried the name, offering her his arm.

"Well, Miss Amelia Sudbury, as I now see you are here in search of my sister and not to trespass, allow me to escort you inside."

Amelia looked as if she might like to tuck her arm in his but before she could move her expression turned to disdain once more, and she folded her hands primly at her waist.

"You are very kind, Sir Benjamin, but I assure you I know the way and am quite able to get there myself."

Before Devereaux could say a word, she had turned on her pretty heels and begun to walk quite confidently towards the house. He hurried after her, careful to keep a respectable distance between them, and yet all the same not as eager to draw their interview to a hasty close as she seemed to be.

"You are in the habit of letting yourself into other people's houses, are you, Miss Sudbury?"

"I shall do no such thing!" she cried, indignant. "I intend to ring the bell just as any other visitor would."

"Ah, you prefer to wait on the cold doorstep for the housekeeper than to be escorted in on the arm of the master of the house."

She fixed him with a look that would have been withering, had Ben not had plenty of practice at enduring scathing glances from young ladies. From most, the expression had little effect, yet in this instance he felt his lips tugging into a smile he struggled, manfully, to hold back.

"You do not seem eager to make my acquaintance, Miss Sudbury," he continued, after they had walked a moment in silence, she taking two steps for every one of his, and yet not quite managing to outpace him. "I can only speculate as to the reason for your reticence -"

"Reticence? Sir Benjamin, you mistake me," she said, her voice coming out a little breathless on account of the exertion of her progress towards the sanctuary of the house. "I am merely eager to see my friend again. When last we parted she was not quite herself and I wish to be assured of her wellbeing."

"Then allow me to ease your concerns, Miss Sudbury. My sister is quite well, and entirely at ease with my presence here at home." He smiled wolfishly at her and was gratified to see that her eyes, once they met his, did not dart away quite as quickly as they had done before. "I assume it was the threat of my arrival that rendered poor Jo *not quite herself* when last you were together?"

The ghost of a frown skirted across Miss Sudbury's delicate features, and Devereaux checked himself. The use of his baby sister's pet name had escaped him, for though she was quite fully grown now, and a young lady after the pattern of the very one before him, she would still always be the same roly-poly Jo, who had called him "Dev" and hung onto his tails whenever he was home from school. It was his turn to frown, for in the intervening years her affection for him had waned into something that might have been hatred. He dropped his gaze to the ground. No wonder this Miss Sudbury, his sister's particular friend, was reluctant to know him. She must have heard the same rumours as his sister - rumours her own mother was responsible for.

"Well, I very much doubt you will care to accept my word on the subject, however truthful I may promise it to be." He drew himself to a stop, bowing stiffly, and bid Miss Sudbury a cold farewell. "I would not wish to interrupt your reunion by my presence, and so shall return to my task. As you declare, you seem well acquainted with the property and I am sure my sister will be only too pleased to see you once more. Good day."

He turned and stalked away, wondering just how many introductions he would make that had been tainted by his stepmother.

Chapter Four

"Have you seen him?" Joanna had barely greeted Amelia before she launched into a discussion of her brother's merits, of which there were but few, and his faults, which seemed innumerable.

"He is handsome, I suppose," she said, reflecting upon Devereaux's dark hair and even, regal countenance. She slipped her arm through Amelia's and led her in a slow circuit of the large Roland parlour. "And doesn't he know it! One cannot fault his manners, but oh! The things he has done! I cannot bear to tell you!"

Amelia rather wished Joanna *would* tell her, for she felt as if she could do with a hearty reminder of just how bad the handsome Sir Benjamin was, in order to quell the very natural response she had had to meeting him by chance in the grounds of the house she knew so well.

"He - he has arrived recently?" she ventured, at last, when Joanna paused for breath.

"Yesterday. And already he roams about as if he owned the place!"

"But, my dear, he does, does he not?"

Joanna's eyes flashed dangerously and for a moment she looked not unlike the brother she claimed to despise. Amelia swallowed the thought, feeling sure that her friend would not thank her for making such a comparison.

"That is, I dare say he merely wishes to become reacquainted with Roland Park and its environs. It is quite some time since he was last here, is not it?"

"Ten years." Joanna's voice was low, little more than a growl. "He at least had the grace to stay away in that time. He must have known how badly his behaviour reflected upon us as a family -" She stopped short, then, glancing at her friend and endeavouring to change the subject. "I am just sorry you came across him alone. I hope he behaved!"

"He was quite the gentleman," Amelia volunteered, choosing not to mention the wicked grin that had lurked on the handsome face, nor the knowing tone that crept into his voice and made Amelia blush to remember. "I dare say I startled him as much as he did me. I do not think he expected to see a young lady creeping about the grounds uninvited."

"Uninvited? Pah!" Joanna threw herself down on a sofa with such ferocity that Amelia's arm, still nestled in her friend's, tugged her along with the motion. She sat, carefully, next to Joanna and smoothed her skirts.

"Am I not even to be free to have my friends call on me, now that *he* is here?"

Amelia had no answer to this, and her eyes darted around the room, eager for something, anything, to speak of that might settle Joanna's fiery sensibilities.

"Let me tell you of my trials this morning, dear, and we shall speak no longer of Sir Benjamin." She spoke these words carefully, feeling that she, personally, would rather like to speak more of Sir Benjamin, to deduce from Joanna the exact nature of his wrongs, and in particular, what it was that caused him to be exiled from Roland Park, to begin with. She had never yet managed to extract this intelligence from her friend but having met the man who until that day had been but a spectre in her imagination piqued Amelia's curiosity. She knew that Joanna was too ruffled to speak easily, however, and decided to embark instead on a campaign of distraction, telling her friend of her failed errands that morning. The mention of hair-ribbons was the magic elixir that restored Joanna to herself, however, and she seized hold of the subject with enthusiasm.

"I have been rummaging in my scrap-bag for some remnants of lace, myself," she mused, reaching for the bag and giving it a shake so that it rattled with knitting needles and bobbins quite fiercely. "Since *he* arrived, Mama will not permit me to buy anything new, so I am doing all I can to improve the dresses I have for the season." She sighed, filled with self-pity. "I would dearly love something new for the assembly, but that seems an impossible dream now, for Benjamin has absconded with all of Papa's ledgers and locked them in his study until further notice." She scowls. "I think he must be a dreadful miser -"

"I thought him more a spendthrift," Amelia remarked, innocently referencing one of Joanna's long-held grudges against her invisible brother.

"Oh!" Joanna frowned, clearly recalling more than a dozen occasions where she had made just such an accusation against her absent brother. "Yes..." She fumbled. "Yes, indeed he is a spendthrift where his own interests are concerned. One need only to look at his elegant - by which I mean expensive - wardrobe to reach that conclusion. But when it comes to his provision for Mama and me it is different. He will not be generous, I am sure of it." She sniffed. "Mama has barely come out of her room. He has asked to have an audience with her already but she has put him off." She dropped her voice to a whisper. "Poor Mama. She cannot bear to see him when he looks so like Papa."

This was such a surprising comparison - and so untrue, for Amelia had scarcely known two gentlemen to be less alike in appearance - that a laugh bubbled in her chest almost before she could catch it, and Amelia struggled to disguise it as a cough.

"Oh dear, Milly! Are you unwell?" Joanna's preoccupation with her own troubles vanished as she turned sympathetically to her friend. "You ought not to be out walking in this weather! You will surely catch a cold." Her lips turned down at the corners. "If you haven't already done so." She leaned back, an action that was surely a reflex, for in the same breath she was offering to summon a servant to make up a bed for her and request a carriage to convey her home, whichever course of action her *poor, dear friend* would most prefer.

"I am quite well, Joanna, you needn't fret!" Amelia smiled broadly as if to demonstrate the cough was nothing more than a cough, without betraying that it had, in fact, been a fiction.

The clock on the mantel chimed, and Amelia seized upon it as an excuse to draw their interview to a close. Whilst she was reluctant to part from her friend, she rather wanted to be left alone to her thoughts, to shuffle through the jumble of conflicting notions she had of the newly-arrived Sir Benjamin in the hope she might be able to construct one full, useful picture of him. She could not begin to do such a thing with the man's sister sitting not two feet away from her.

"I ought to bid you farewell and continue towards home. I only intended on making but the briefest of calls here and Papa will be beginning to worry about me."

This was certainly a falsehood because Admiral Sudbury rarely had cause to fret over his forthright daughter, giving her almost all the freedom he would have afforded a son, much to the ladies of Westham's concern, and Amelia's freedom-loving delight.

"Oh." Joanna straightened. "Well, at least let me send for a carriage. You should have an escort -"

"No!" At the mention of the word *escort*, Amelia recalled Sir Benjamin's offer to be just such a one himself, and she did not wish to afford him a second opportunity to offer, where she would be less free to refuse. "Do not worry, dear. I am quite happy walking."

Joanna cast a glance towards the window, her eyebrows lifting.

"I know you love to be out of doors, Milly, but have you not noticed that it is raining? You certainly cannot mean to walk home in a deluge. No, I will not allow it." She rubbed her hands together as if the natural world itself had conspired to keep her friend at her mercy a little while longer. "Stay and take tea with me. Perhaps, by the time we are done, the weather will have eased, and then you may continue your walk."

Amelia smiled, faintly, seeing she had no argument to offer in objection to this, and feeling, with a wary glance towards the door, that perhaps she would be better served to remain here in the parlour in the company of her friend, than to risk tramping about the grounds of Roland Park alone just at present.

⁘

THE HEAVENS HAD OPENED precisely at the moment that Devereaux was at the furthest reaches of his property. *Of course.* At first, he had sought shelter beneath a tree, but when a crack of thunder suggested first, that such a shelter might not be the wisest course of action and second, that the rain was likely to endure for more than a moment or two, he abandoned the attempt, and strode instead towards home, his feet squelching in his boots and his clothes becoming increasingly sodden and heavy.

A dog barked and he glanced up, squinting through the sheeting rain to see Smith, the groundskeeper, walking merrily towards him, an excited dog running circles around his heels, and barking gleefully at Ben. Neither man nor beast paid any heed to the rain.

"Fine weather we are having today," he growled, as the man drew close enough to make conversation.

"Aye, it's certainly a little inclement." Smith raked a hand through his sodden hair, sending drops of water in all directions. "But it'll do the ground good. I wonder, Sir Benjamin if I might speak to you later. I have a few concerns about the stables and some suggestions for modifications." He grimaced. "I'd not have chosen to talk to you in the middle of a downpour, but -"

"Fine." A fat raindrop chose that moment to drop down Ben's neck making him flinch, and he began to walk again.

"Find me later." He shot an angry look at the darkening skies. "Indoors."

"Will do." Smith whistled, calling back his dog, who was busy circling Ben once more. "Good afternoon, Sir Benjamin."

"Good afternoon." Devereaux stalked towards the house, feeling more wet and miserable with every step. After what seemed like an age he reached the entrance and had begun shedding his sodden clothing almost before he crossed the threshold, caring only to get free of the heavy, ice-cold layers.

"Sir Benjamin!" the housekeeper squeaked, hurrying towards him and retrieving each item from where he had dropped it. "Are you quite well, sir?"

"I am soaking, Mrs Henderson, but other than that, yes, quite well." He sneezed and rolled his eyes skywards. *Please do not punish me with getting sick the very instant I arrive in the country!* Lennox would never tire of teasing him about that, constructing some fancy where the town-dwelling Devereaux was so unused to life in the country that a mere day of it had rendered him unwell.

"Find my valet, would you?" he croaked, smoothing his soaking hair back and cringing as rivulets of icy rainwater made their way down his back. "Have him meet me with a fresh change of clothing. And make up the fire in my study." He groaned. "I have a mountain of work to attend to, and will not care to be disturbed until dinner."

A musical laugh distracted him, then, and he paused in his progress, glancing around as if he could deduce, by looking, where it came from.

"Miss Devereaux is in the parlour, Sir Benjamin," Mrs Henderson said, dropping a quick curtsey and snatching up his cravat from where it lay in a puddle on the floor. "And Miss Sudbury with her. I dare say Miss Sudbury will be with us for the duration, sir. Shall I plan on setting an extra seat at the dining table?"

Benjamin nodded, dismissing the woman with a wave, and, despite being half-clothed and fully soaked, could not help but draw a little closer to the parlour door. It was open a crack and he positioned himself that he might observe the room's occupants without himself being seen, discerning two heads bent over a crackling fire. Both young ladies were working at some bit of knitting or needlework and they talked as they worked, their voices soft and light and filled with affection for one another. They made such a pretty picture that it was all Ben could do to keep himself from pushing the door open and joining them. It was not until a cold breeze found him that he remembered himself and turned away from the room, determined to change and then see to his work, which would occupy the best part of the afternoon. His sister would not thank him for intruding on her time with her friend, and that friend...

He smirked, recalling his first meeting with Miss Amelia Sudbury. He very much doubted *she* would be glad of his presence, either. Yet that thought did not entirely disappoint him, for he felt, in some region of his torso that might have been his heart, that her reluctance to see him would be at least partly feigned. He was not unaware of his more attractive qualities, and whilst he had not showcased them to their greatest benefit, he might yet succeed in winning Miss Sudbury's heart, with or without her meaning him to.

He climbed the stairs two at a time, the plan that was already forming in his mind giving energy to his steps. At dinner that evening, for instance, he might succeed in being his most charming self and quite disprove whatever rumours and speculation Josie's young friend currently believed true of him. He swallowed a laugh, rather relishing the thought that he might so easily do away with the villainous image she had conjured and settle in its place a handsome, charming gentleman, poised to sweep in and turn Westham on its head.

As he passed his stepmother's rooms, he thought he heard footsteps and his mood darkened. She still had not deigned to speak to him. *Deigned to, or dared to!* Surely she must know that he was aware of the falsehoods she had told about him. His father had not minced his words when he sent the young Devereux away, and rumours had a way of reaching the ears of those they concerned, regardless of their content.

He paused, raising his hand to the heavy oak door, and knocked. Straining to listen, he heard her sudden intake of breath and decided to speak anyway, though the door remained closed.

"Lady Devereaux," he called. "I trust you are recovering from this particular bout of ill-health. I would like to formally request your presence at dinner this evening. It appears Josie has a friend who will be joining us, so you need not fear my behaviour on this particular occasion." A grim smile crept onto his features, giving his voice a strange light. "I will be every inch a gentleman, and trust you will acquit yourself in the way only a lady can. We will dine at eight o'clock."

He did not wait for her response, but turned directly toward his own room, feeling anticipation rise in his chest at the evening that lay ahead of them. He might kill two birds with one stone, and smooth out his future in Westham as well as undoing some of the damage from his past.

Chapter Five

A t last the rain began to ease and Amelia decided she might return home. She had scarcely reached the door to the parlour when it flew open and she found herself faced, once more, with Sir Benjamin Devereaux.

"You are not leaving, are you, Miss Sudbury? Surely our hospitality is not so dire that you wish to leave it so soon." He clapped his hands. "No, I have already arranged it: you will stay to dine with us."

This was uttered with such confidence that it took Amelia a moment to digest his words, and a moment longer to respond.

"Oh, Sir Benjamin, you are very kind." She darted a glance over her shoulder towards Joanna, who was watching their interaction with practised poise. Only her unnaturally wide eyes suggested that she was straining to discern every word that passed between the pair. "Alas, I cannot stay, however much I might wish to. My father..."

"Has already been informed of the change to your plans." Devereaux smiled, the perfect combination of warmth and danger. Amelia felt her stomach flip and clamped her arms over it as an extra barrier against further betrayal. Her mind, if not her body, knew to withstand this charm.

"It did not occur to you to *ask* me, before arranging my evening to suit your own household?"

Amelia was shocked at her own bravery. In fact, it seemed to her at that moment that it was not her speaking at all, but some other braver young lady. She heard Joanna's breath catch.

"It did not occur to me that you should prefer to eat in the company of an ageing admiral, rather than with friends," Devereaux said smoothly. His smile fell a little on the last word, his eyes darting over Amelia's shoulder towards his sister, and back again. "Or one friend, at least." He tilted his chin. "You did mention you were concerned for my sister's wellbeing, did you not? How better to ascertain it than over the course of a meal?"

He said nothing more but his eyes remained fixed on her, a mocking stare that said more than mere words would have managed. *Are your motives not as pure as you claim? Perhaps you came here only to investigate my rumoured return.* There was a challenge in those eyes, yes, and something else too. Some light that Amelia had not noticed when she spoke to him first, something that disappeared again almost as soon as she had noticed it was there so that she was left to second-guess her noticing it at all.

"Very well," she murmured, disinclined at that moment to argue more or to stand by a firm refusal that would harm her as much as her hosts. She glanced towards the window. It was indeed growing dark, and whilst the rain had ceased there was a damp chill in the air that she did not relish the thought of walking in.

"I'm sorry, Miss. Sudbury, I did not hear you?"

The wolfish smile was back, the voice just as smooth as she remembered. Tossing her head so that her curls bounced, she forced a taut smile onto her features, and repeated her words, loud enough that even her father might hear, miles away and taking dinner, as he would be, in his study.

"I said *very well*, Sir Benjamin. I accept your invitation to dine here this evening. You are very kind."

"Kind?" Devereaux waved away the word with an expression that was almost mocking. "I have been called a great many things, Miss Sudbury, in these walls and outside of them. I doubt very much that *kind* was amongst them. I invite you as a favour to my sister." He turned his attention to the hearth. "You see, Joanna? I am not here solely to plague you, *whatever your Mama has to say on the matter.*"

This last was murmured in little more than a low growl and Amelia wondered if he had intended to say the words aloud at all.

"Perhaps - perhaps you will join us, Sir Benjamin," she blurted, not quite sure where the invitation had come from. It provoked a muffled gasp from her friend, and the same sly smile crept back over Devereaux's handsome face.

"Ah, I see how it is. You object to me running my own household, Miss Sudbury, but now you wish to order me about within it. You know there is but one woman who has the authority to tell me what to do in my own home."

"Yes, of course, I am so sorry, I only meant -" Amelia stammered, her cheeks flushing from embarrassment. She tried to move away from him, back towards the fireplace where she might blame her flaming cheeks on the heat of the fire and not her proximity to him.

"Mama will not mind it," Joanna asserted, lifting her own chin in an imperious, unconscious mirror of her brother. "She has always wished for me and my friends to feel quite at home here."

"I'm quite sure she has," Devereaux said, lazily. He strolled further into the room, passing Amelia with very little space so that she could smell the spicy scent of his cologne, feel the transitory heat of his body as he moved through the space nearest her. With a grunt, he collapsed on a sofa, kicking his long legs out and crossing them at the ankle. "But when I refer to the one lady - and one lady, only, mind - I will tolerate ordering me about in my own home I certainly do not refer to *your Mama*, Josie." His eyes fluttered closed, the ghost of a smile still playing about his lips. "Nor to you, before you begin to get ideas. No, the only woman I shall alllow to direct my steps is my wife."

There was a collective intake of breath at this, and Amelia glanced at Joanna, certain that her own expression was likewise horrified. *Sir Benjamin Devereaux - married? And where, then, was his wife? Was there no end to the scandal the man wore, like a well-tailored suit?*

"I wondered what it was that would silence the tongues of inquisitive young misses," he mused, stifling a yawn. "Had I known I needed only to mention a wife I would have done so months ago."

He opened his eyes suddenly and swiftly fixed them on Amelia.

"Alas, she as at present still nought but a name. *My wife*. She does not exist except in theory."

The words were wistful, almost, but before Amelia could wonder about it, he had spoken again, in the clipped, sharp tone that brought her wondering to a swift conclusion.

"And so, Miss Sudbury, you will forgive me if I choose to ignore any attempt you, or any other lady, make in ordering me about, this or any other evening."

DEVEREAUX LAPSED INTO silence and closed his eyes, allowing his sister and Miss Sudbury to think he was sleeping. In truth, he was not far from it. The warmth of the fire and the comforting murmur of female voices lulled him into a state of not-quite-wakefulness. A word caught his ear, but he remained as he was with his eyes closed, enjoying the freedom afforded him by the semblance of sleep. The young ladies ignored him, chattering with a freedom they would not have enjoyed had they suspected him to be listening.

Assembly. That had been the word that caught Ben's ear and set his mind racing. He had forgotten how much of a highlight these social gatherings could be in the country. In London, it seemed as if there were balls and dances held every other week, not to mention enough lectures, dinners, club nights and general outings amongst his set that one need never spend an evening alone unless one wished. He grimaced, faintly, recalling how even desire was never a guarantee of solitude. How often had he ended up playing host to Lennox and their shared acquaintances after crying off an evening's entertainments? But here, in the countryside, such opportunities for dancing must be few and far between and the promise of a gathering afforded his sister and Miss Sudbury all manner of excited speculations.

"Her cousin."

"No!"

"Truly! He is here visiting them, although I hear he is worth three thousand a year and is looking for an estate of his own."

"I wonder what traits they share." This was Joanna, who giggled as she spoke. "Imagine him with poor Maryanne's nose! Or the same long neck as Jane."

"I am sure, for three thousand a year you might learn to appreciate even the homeliest of appearances!" Amelia said, tutting good-naturedly.

"For three thousand? Not I!" Joanna snorted. "Perhaps for five, or ten..."

The girls collapsed into whispered laughter, brought to a sudden still when Ben pretended to snore, sinking his shoulders further into the plush upholstery of his seat. There was a moment's quiet whilst they paused to reassure themselves of his apparent slumber, and then they continued.

"Well, we can't all be like *you*, Milly!" Joanna hissed. "Clinging to ideals of love and romance." His sister's voice was scathing, and Ben cracked one eye open a fraction to see Amelia's smile fall, momentarily, before she rallied, squaring her shoulders and dismissing Joanna's disparagement with a philosophical shrug.

"I would rather be a spinster than wedded to disappointment."

"They are one and the same!" Joanna exclaimed in a stage whisper. "You will spend your days keeping house for the

Admiralty, I suppose. Can you not persuade your brother to bring home some eligible captain or other?"

Amelia shuddered.

"I certainly do not intend to marry one of Arthur's friends. You forget, Josie, that I have known them all for years, and they me. They are good men, all, but one can scarcely converse for more than a minute with any of them on a topic not related to their ship!"

"And why such need of conversation?" Joanna would not be so easily discouraged. "You put far too much stock in talking. I would be quite content to marry an idiot, provided he adored me."

"And was in possession of a fortune."

"Well, of course!" Joanna laughed. "I should *like* a title, too, but as we have seen, that is no guarantee of gentlemanly conduct." She sniffed, haughtily, and Devereaux felt certain she had directed this particular comment in his direction. Miss Sudbury made no reply, and Ben was not sure whether to feel amused or disappointed that she did not come to his defence. He held his breath, wondering what his sister would say next. He scarcely recognised roly-poly Jo in the elegant young lady before him and wished there was some way to broach the distance between them, but he was at a loss as to what. She was predisposed to dislike him. Her mother had seen to that.

"Mama says..." Joanna began, and Ben strained to hear what amounted to little more than a whisper, feeling as if his fleeting thought of Lady Devereaux had conjured a reference to her from her daughter's lips.

"Mama says he cannot mean to stay for long. He will miss London and soon be on his way back there."

"London!" Miss Sudbury said the words with reverence.

"I know! If only the name of *Devereaux* were not so well known there on account of his misdeeds, I might convince Mama to let me have a season there. She will not set foot there, now, for all our good reputation has been tarnished by association."

"He cannot be so very bad, surely?" Amelia ventured, and Benjamin felt his heart lift. One young lady in all of Westham was willing to give him the benefit of the doubt. His hopes were crushed as Joanna began to list off his sins in a resigned tone.

"Well, there is the gambling, of course. And he runs with such a wild set." Her voice dropped again and Ben was forced to adjust his posture, angling his ear a little closer to the ladies so that he stood a chance of hearing his sister's words. "Mr Merriweather. Mr Lennox. Mr Stephens." Her voice grew dark. "They are referred to throughout London as *the four horsemen*. You know, of the apocalypse. That is the sort of havoc they wreak wherever they go. And, of course, the business with Mary was what began it all -" She froze, then, and he heard the sound of a hand being clamped over her mouth. "Oh! But I wasn't supposed to mention it. Oh, Milly, please. You must not tell Mama that I told you. She will be furious!"

Ben scarcely heard a word of Amelia's response, if indeed she gave one at all, for his thoughts had been utterly consumed by the mention of Mary, whose presence had been so thoroughly consigned to his past that it quite stunned him to hear her mentioned again, and in this house.

"You can trust me," Amelia whispered. I shan't say a word. Oh!" She had turned as she spoke, leaning to set her teacup down on a small end-table but had misjudged its edge, and the teacup slid towards the ground. Quick as a flash, Ben darted his hand forward, catching it before it hit the solid wood floor and smashed. His action averted disaster, the cup was saved, but his own deception was revealed and as he returned the rescued cup and saucer to the table he was faced with two pairs of shocked, scornful eyes, and he did the only thing he could think of to bring the situation to a conclusion. He smiled the same brazen smile that had got him out of a dozen scrapes and landed him in half a dozen more.

"Well, ladies. If you have quite finished discussing my misdeeds, both real and imagined, perhaps we ought to go in to dinner."

Chapter Six

Amelia had hardly dared to look at Sir Benjamin Devereaux again as the small party made their way into the dining room. Had he been listening to them the whole time? That he would lull them into thinking he was asleep so that he might listen, secretly, to their conversation struck her as a dreadful deceit, but she supposed she ought not to be surprised. He was surely capable of any wrongdoing.

She and Joanna walked in tandem a few paces behind Devereaux and both girls were so lost in their thoughts that neither one noticed him come to a halt at the bottom of the stairs.

"Oof!"

"Ouch!"

Amelia had collided with his back and hurried back a step, her cheeks flaming with heat and embarrassment. Joanna had made the same mistake and both young ladies looked at him a little sheepishly.

Devereaux, for his part, was merely amused. He opened his mouth to make another comment in that smooth, teasing voice of his, but before he could speak, a movement on the stairs caught his eye.

"Ah, Lady Devereaux. I'm glad you have decided to join us for dinner."

Joanna's breath caught, and Amelia glanced towards her momentarily before lifting her gaze towards Lady Devereaux.

Amelia had always found Joanna's mother a little intimidating. Tall and almost painfully thin, she nonetheless had an iron will and constitution and it was she, rather than Joanna's father, who had been the disciplinarian of the house. Today she seemed to be a shadow of her former self as she glided down the stairs.

Devereaux offered her his arm, and Amelia thought she detected a moment of hesitation before Lady Devereaux accepted it. She did not look at him, though, and Amelia wondered if she bore as much of a grudge towards the newly arrived Sir Benjamin as did her daughter.

The party began to move towards the dining room, Sir Benjamin and his stepmother moving stiffly, awkwardly, as if they were strangers. Worse than strangers, for this brittle politeness was more pained than might exist between even the slightest of acquaintances.

"Your mother looks well," she whispered to Joanna, eager to hear her friend's impression of them.

"I am amazed she is joining us!" Joanna admitted, with a scowl at her brother's ramrod straight back. "I expect *he* had something to do with it. He will have forced her hand in some way. See how she keeps a distance between them? I do not blame her! I would not wish to take his arm if I had a choice."

Amelia remembered how hard it had been to resist that particular arm when it was offered to her, and said nothing. She knew that relations between Devereaux and the ladies in his family had been strained and whilst she now had some glimpse into the reason why the details were scant enough that she was forced to fill in the many gaps out of her imagination. *Mary*. She turned the name over in her mind. Who was she? And what had Devereaux done that had been so shameful as to cause his family to banish him and never speak of it again?

Amelia saved her rumination for later, wondering if, at dinner, she might yet glean some more detail that would help her to form an accurate picture of Benjamin Devereaux's past. She could not help her eyes straying to him, now that his attention was otherwise occupied by the lady he escorted into dinner. She had thought it a fact of novels, only, that meant a rake had to be handsome, but Benjamin Devereaux certainly seemed to prove the rule. His dark features, when not obscured by a scowl, were undeniably attractive, although she found herself missing the sly smile that had played about his lips when he spoke to her. His features were blank of all expression now, and she wondered whether it took an effort to remain so inscrutable.

The dining room at Roland Park was not the largest Amelia had ever been in, but it was certainly one of the most elegant. Lit by the warm glow of candles and piled high with food, she tried not to let an expression of wonder rest on her features. Their own dining table at home was not small, but as it usually seated just Amelia and the admiral, there was very little need for elegance. She suddenly felt a little out of place and was only too happy when everybody took their seats and the first course was served.

"I hear there is to be an assembly, soon." It was Devereaux who spoke, although he did not address his observation towards anybody in particular. Amelia waited for Joanna to reply, but her friend's fierce expression was fixed on her plate and, unable to bear the tense silence any longer, Amelia offered a response.

"In Westham proper," she said, taking a sip from her glass.

"And will you attend?"

Devereaux's voice was warm, courteous, and it felt for a moment as if he and Amelia were alone at the table.

"Did you not already hear us say that we would?" Joanna asked, scowling at her dinner plate. "Why ask us questions if you already know the answer?"

"My dear sister, those are the only questions one ought ever to ask." Devereaux's expression had gown sanguine again, his voice languorous and smooth. "It is too much of a risk to ask a question to which one does not already know the answer, do you not agree, Lady Devereaux?"

There was something behind his question, some dig that Amelia could not begin to understand. She looked to Joanna for clarification but her friend merely rolled her eyes as if such a ridiculous comment was only what could be expected from her brother.

"Mama," she began, interrupting her brother's question with one of her own. "I shall not have to wear mourning to the assembly, shall I? I so hate wearing such dreary colours. And do not say I cannot dance or else I shall go mad!"

Silence descended on the table once more at Joanna's mention of mourning which must have led every mind present to the immediate recollection of what it was that had brought their fractured family together: the death of its patriarch.

"You must do whatever you think appropriate." Lady Devereaux had spoken for the first time that evening, and Amelia was surprised to find that she did not sound unlike her old self. She had half-expected her voice to be strained from crying but now she seemed almost entirely unchanged. Quieter, yes, and her movements were still more measured, but had she not been clad head to toe in black and had Amelia not been aware she had spent the past week keeping to her room she might not have known there was anything wrong with her at all.

Her answer, though, was precisely what Joanna had wished for, and she turned to Amelia, a smile brightening her delicate features.

"I suppose you will be wanting a new dress, in that case." Devereaux's low voice bore a trace of mocking amusement, but before Amelia could wonder at it, Joanna had brazenly answered in the affirmative.

"I expect you shall think me frivolous, *brother*, but considering the ways you have been known to waste money I do not think it unreasonable to desire a new dress for the only assembly I shall attend all winter!"

Amelia carefully laid down her fork, bracing for what would surely be an explosion of temper. Indeed, a fire raged in Sir Benjamin's dark eyes, and even Joanna's false confidence seemed to falter a little in the face of the glare he fixed upon her. It was a surprise to all present, then, when he threw his head back and laughed.

"VERY WELL, *sister*," Devereaux put the same pointed inflexion on the title as Joanna had used when addressing him. "You shall have your new dress. And perhaps we might venture a little further afield than Westham to procure it." He wrinkled his nose. He had not made it as far as the small town since his return home but he recalled it well enough from his youth and doubted it had changed greatly in the intervening years. "Perhaps your friend would care to accompany us?"

This was uttered in a light, off-hand fashion but whilst Ben strove to conceal his true feelings regarding this suggestion, he could not entirely hide his motivations from his own self. He was intrigued by Miss Amelia Sudbury and hoped she would say yes so that he might be afforded an opportunity to get to know her better before the looming promise of the assembly. She did not like him but as she did not yet know him he felt quite confident of his abilities to change this. He had won enough admirers and broken enough hearts to be well aware of his power over the gentler sex. He found his eyes drawn, despite himself, to Joanna's companion and railed inwardly that her expression remained almost entirely unreadable.

"Where to?" Joanna's eyes widened and an excited smile rested momentarily on her features before she appeared to recall precisely whom she had to thank for the suggestion and wiped her expression, returning it to something neutral. "I suppose I might benefit from a visit further afield, to Malton, perhaps. Provided, of course, that Amelia wishes to come with us." She turned to her friend so that Ben's view of either young lady was obstructed. "Won't you come?"

She had asked the words so naturally, yet they were precisely the words *he* had longed to ask in so easy a manner. He was not sure he was even capable of addressing a young lady with such normalcy. He found his ears attuned to the slightest noise Miss Sudbury made and did not move a muscle until she replied.

"I am not sure whether my father can spare me," she said at last, and if Devereaux felt a wave of disappointment roll through him he certainly made no appearance of it. Joanna was not so stoical.

"Not spare you?" she cried. "Why, we are only talking of a few hours, Milly! I am quite sure the admiral will be more than capable of doing without you for an afternoon. And he might even thank us for freeing him from the chore of dealing with *ribbon and lace and other nonsense*, as I have heard him refer to the particulars of feminine dress on more than one occasion!"

Ben shifted in his seat so that his eyes could rest on Amelia's face undisturbed, and he saw a muscle twitch in her cheek that suggested that this was a direct quote from the lips of Admiral Sudbury. He recalled the reluctance in her voice when she and Joanna were speaking together in the parlour and wondered if it was her father's lack of interest, and not any lack of funds, that made the prospect of a new dress something almost unreachable for the pretty Miss Sudbury.

"I will ask him," Amelia promised, returning to her dinner. This would have to satisfy his sister, as it did Benjamin, who made a private promise that he would do all he could to ensure the admiral ruled in their favour, whether Miss Sudbury would thank him for his assistance or not. It would be a kindness to Joanna to have her friend with her and it was for his sister's sake, not his own, that he made a private pledge to act.

"Good." Ben pushed his plate aside. "I have some business to attend to this week. Perhaps we can combine the two."

At the mention of *business* Lady Devereaux sniffed, the very gesture he had seen so often deployed against him by her daughter, and he raised his eyes mockingly toward her.

"You are welcome to accompany us too, *Mama.*" He stole Joanna's name for her, for Lady Devereaux had never in his life been *Mama*. Even *Mother* had felt foreign to the young Ben, and he had dropped the moniker as soon as he was able, referring to her by her title if he referred to her at all. He recalled his own mother, a hazy image tinged with light, and wondered, not for the first time, how different his life and his father's might have been had she not succumbed so early to illness.

"I do not think it right that I am seen out and about on so frivolous an errand whilst still in mourning for my husband," Lady Devereaux said, meeting his gaze unflinchingly.

Ben arched an eyebrow.

"Indeed. I suppose calling on one's friends in the neighbourhood does not count as a *frivolous errand,* such that it might be accomplished mere hours after my father's demise, whilst picking up a pen to write to me was too great a challenge." He shrugged his broad shoulders, ignoring the chorus of gasps that came from the young ladies seated at the table. "No matter. I well understand your reluctance to spend money that you are no longer entitled to. I applaud you for it, in fact. I suppose you will choose not to attend the assembly at all, in that case, but keep close to home."

Lady Devereaux bit her lip and Ben could tell she was carefully weighing her response, trying to decide how best to address the notion that yes, she had planned to attend the assembly, clad in expensive mourning and courting a sympathetic audience from her neighbours while she continued to sow seeds of dislike about her newly arrived step-son.

"Oh, you may come, Mama, mayn't she, Amelia?" Joanna turned a plaintive expression towards her friend. "It is not so very shocking that a lady in mourning attend a social event, provided she does not dance -"

"I would not like to speak for your mother," Amelia said, softly. "But I recall, when Mama died, that Father could scarcely be encouraged to leave the house for months." She swallowed, as if even the memory of so dark a time in her life caused her fresh pain now. Ben felt a strange compulsion to reach out to her, to prove by some gesture that he, too, understood the painful loss of a parent, of having one's life forever shifted. Instead, he laced his fingers together, bringing them to his chin meditatively, while he listened to Amelia's quiet words.

"I do not know how anyone can ever imagine life to go on at all when one has lost someone one loves so very dearly."

Chapter Seven

A s the evening drew to a close Amelia was surprised to acknowledge a sense of disappointment. She was even more surprised to confess, although she would not do so aloud, that she had enjoyed dining with the Devereauxs. She confided as much in the pages of her journal, which she had attended to as she clambered into bed that evening, by the light of a candle that flickered in the cold night air.

I ought to go to sleep! she thought, yawning into the back of her hand. *I shall just finish this page...* Her pen travelled quickly over the paper, recalling the way the light had danced across Sir Benjamin's handsome features, the precise timbre of his voice and how it changed when he addressed his sister, his stepmother, and her. She shivered and automatically reached to pull her blankets a little tighter. Surely she had only imagined that his voice changed when he addressed himself to her, and yet she did not see how she could have dreamt up such a detail. Certainly, his whole manner was different when he addressed Lady Devereaux. Amelia had known the two were not fond of one another and from the few clues that Joanna had dropped she had been firmly on the side of Lady Devereaux, despite her own mixed feelings towards that lady. One evening in the company of Sir Benjamin, and she was in danger of forming an entirely new opinion. Devereaux had been compassionate, kind even. *I am sure you have heard me called a great many things, Miss Sudbury, in these walls and outside of them. I doubt very much that kind was amongst them.* She bit her lip as the memory of Devereaux's words brought back the memory of his face as he had said them.

I suppose it is a necessity that a man who seeks to build the reputation of a rake must be handsome, she reasoned, slipping the ribbon she used as a marker between the pages of her journal and sliding the book closed. *But is it a necessity that he be quite* so *handsome?*

She coloured at this thought, though there was nobody in the room to witness it and nobody alive who could know it. Except, perhaps, for Devereaux himself. The way he had smirked at her had suggested he knew precisely what thoughts ran through her mind at any given time, which infuriated her and made her all the more determined to trip him up. *I am not like the young ladies you usually associate with, Sir Benjamin,* she thought, summoning up the image of his smirking, handsome face to direct her silent comment to. She was no delicate flower, poised to wilt under the slightest glimmer of attention. She would not seek it out, either, for whilst she had never yet been to London or experienced *the season,* she had read novels enough to imagine that there were untold scores of young ladies eager to secure Sir Benjamin's wealth and title - now that he was in possession of them both - for their own. Perhaps those young women were even happy to endure the behaviour that had qualified him as one-quarter of the notorious four horsemen, but she, Amelia Sudbury, was not. She would rather keep her self-respect, even if it kept her alone all her days.

"I do not care to marry," she whispered aloud, as if hearing the words would make them truer. "Unless I find a gentleman who matches me with wit as well as wealth." She pursed her lips. Unfortunately, in her albeit limited experience, she had met gentlemen possessing only one or the other. And now, at last, she might have found one in Sir Benjamin who was both clever and rich, and yet he had no morals.

She leaned over the side of the bed, blowing sharply to extinguish her candle and plunging the room into darkness.

If it is morality I want, I suppose I ought to take Father's advice and settle for Mr Connelly. She lifted her hand to her lips to smother a sleepy laugh. The curate *was* a kind man, and certainly must be clever. He did not seem quite capable of matching her wits, though, such that she had abandoned all attempts to goad him into it. Admiral Sudbury merely wanted his only daughter to be happy and he had deduced, from what quarter she could not tell, that no woman could possibly be happy who was not married. With his wife gone and lacking any feminine confidante he might defer the task to, he sought to solve the matter himself and thus pursued a friendship with the curate that brought that young man often to their home, in hopes that lightning would strike and Amelia might magically find herself wed. She did not think her father was particularly partial to the curate more than any other man, but as he was the only gentleman in the admiral's acquaintance under the age of forty, he had decided upon him as the most likely candidate for Amelia's heart.

I suppose I should be grateful, she thought, drowsily. *Papa's circle of gentleman acquaintances is so very narrow. Just think, if he had met Sir Benjamin first, what hope would there be for me?*

But the thought, once formed, was not as amusing as she had expected it to be. She could not quite pinpoint what the heavy feeling of disappointment meant that lodged in her chest, but it was some time before she finally surrendered fully to a dreamless, exhausted sleep.

DEVEREAUX SAT UP LONG after the rest of the house had turned in for the night. He was not sure he would ever get used to the early hours kept by those in the country. In London, at about the time both Joanna and Lady Devereaux talked of retiring for the night, he and his friends would just have been beginning their evening.

He was sprawled in a chair in the study that had belonged to his father and was now his favourite room in the house, on account that it was the one place he was guaranteed of finding sanctuary from the whispers and stares of the servants and the two ladies.

He ought to consider retiring himself, for the fire had died down to its embers, and the air had a cold nip to it, but he could not bring himself to move just yet. How Lennox would tease him for going to bed as early as a child. How Merriweather would sling a companionable arm around him and steer him towards the liquor cabinet, urging him to take just one more drink before bidding the night farewell.

He let out a long, low sigh. He had not anticipated how much he would miss his three friends. He had not anticipated missing them at all! But ten years had proved habit-forming, and he saw the other three *horsemen* on a near daily cycle, individually or in some combination. His eyes darkened. He despised the moniker, and he was less than delighted that this, too, had preceded him to Westham. He wished he really was a horseman, then he might stand a chance of out-riding his reputation.

This sparked an idea in his brains which were not quite yet dulled by lethargy. He would go riding! It had been some time since he had been free to ride with abandon, and he had missed the feel of the wind whipping through his dark hair. It would allow him the chance to avoid his stepmother if he spent much of tomorrow out of doors. He grimaced. She had acquiesced to his request and joined them for dinner but she still had not spoken to him beyond what was strictly necessary. He kicked at the air, wishing he could somehow will her to work with him in this situation his father had left for them to resolve. They were in limbo living here all together in the house that now belonged to him. He knew she expected him to return home and promptly have her and her daughter evicted, and part of him approved of the plan. He could enjoy the privileges of his own house without having to perpetually look over his shoulder. But would that not be as good as admitting he was precisely who everybody expected him to be? Never mind a horseman, he was the antichrist himself, if his stepmother was to be believed. His scowl deepened. She would have people think such evil of him. He knew she was responsible for creating the rumours about him and yet who would believe her capable of them?

Hauling himself to his feet he stretched, lifted his candle and made his way wearily to the door. He did not care what these country folk thought of him, not really. A sharp pain registered in the region of his chest, and he absently reached up to brush at it, as if it were a physical thing. He *ought not to* care about what these country folk thought of him, and for the most part he did not. An ephemeral image of Amelia Sudbury floated behind his eyes, stopping him in his tracks. She, perhaps more than any of the others, was poised to dislike him on account of her friendship with this house. Who knew what Joanna had told her about him and what she believed to be true. He did not know why it bothered him that she thought him a rake or a rogue or some otherwise deplorable human creature, but it did.

He shrugged off the image of Amelia Sudbury and walked slowly upstairs. A floorboard creaked ahead of him and he paused, blinking blearily into the darkness. He held his candle aloft and almost fell back when the light illuminated a figure. He caught hold of the bannister at the last minute, righting himself.

"Oh, it's you," he muttered, dismissing the shadow of his stepmother. He was in no mood to be polite to her at this hour, nor was there anybody nearby to witness him doing so. "What do you want?" he growled, before moderating his voice into something a little friendlier. "Is something the matter?"

"I did as you asked," Lady Devereaux murmured. "I joined you for dinner. Now, will you tell me what fate you have in store for my daughter and me?"

Did he imagine it or did her voice quaver as she spoke? He leaned a little closer, peering up at her and realised that her drawn features were not entirely an affectation. She might not mourn the loss of his father - for he certainly doubted her affection for him had been as genuine as was her affection for his wealth and position - but she was not indifferent to the changes that had taken place. No, it was worse than that. She was...afraid.

A wry laugh bubbled up in Ben's chest.

"You find my pain amusing?" she asked, her voice little more than a sob.

"I find it amusing that our positions have now been reversed, Madam," he said, dipping his head in a feigned bow. "When you sought to see me expelled from my home - very well done, by the way - you cared little for my feelings on the matter. Any worry you feel for your own future, now that it is in my hands to decide, is of your own making." He yawned and did not try to hide it. "I am no monster, Lady Devereaux, no matter what your testimony would have my father, my sister, the entirety of Westham believe. I will not leave you penniless." His breath caught. "But I am still wading through my father's affairs. If you are expecting an answer before the week is out then I am afraid I must disappoint you. Believe me, Madam, I am no more appreciative of this living limbo than you are. I will seek to resolve it as soon as I can. Now, if you will excuse me, I think I will take my leave. I have a busy day planned for the morrow."

Lady Devereaux's breath caught, and he could tell it was on the tip of her tongue to inquire what plans would keep him busy and might they have some effect on her own future and that of her daughter. She wanted to ask, but she would not, and Ben felt no desire to tell her.

"Good night, Dever - Sir Benjamin. I trust you will sleep well." His stepmother's voice was little more than a whisper, but Ben did not stop to acknowledge her words nor to return them.

Chapter Eight

Breakfast at home was almost always a silent affair, with the admiral devoting his attention entirely to his plate and Amelia dividing hers between her meal and her book. Most mornings, her food was neglected in favour of finding out what would happen next to one or other beloved character. That morning, however, neither book nor breakfast was attended to with much enthusiasm, for her lack of sleep afflicted her sorely.

"Dear me, Amelia!" Admiral Sudbury remarked when she yawned for the fourth or fifth time in quick succession. "I wonder if I ought to put my foot down about your gallivanting if it leaves you so weary. And you were not home particularly late last evening, were you?" His eyes twinkled. "Or perhaps it was merely the excitement you experienced at Roland Park. Tell me, have you met the dread *Sir Benjamin* yet?"

Amelia took a sudden interest in the contents of her plate, so that her answer, when it came, was scarcely more than a whisper.

"I assume you already know the answer, Papa. It was he who wrote to tell you that I was staying for dinner, was not it?"

"Indeed it was!" The admiral beamed. "And indeed, I did already suppose that you had met - but after all, one ought never to ask a question to which one does not already know the answer."

Amelia flinched at hearing these words again on her father's lips so soon after she had heard them on Devereaux's. Her fork clattered noisily to the table, and in her eagerness to catch it, she let go the hand that had held open her book, which closed itself mercilessly, losing her place.

"Is something the matter?" Admiral Sudbury grew concerned, a frown darkening his usually merry features. "You do not quite seem yourself this morning, my dear." His frown deepened. "I hope Sir Benjamin was not the terror you imagined. I might say his penmanship betrayed no beastly tendencies. It was altogether a very nice little note and I thought, as his sister and mother would be there also, there was no harm in allowing you to remain. Perhaps I ought to have come myself to collect you -"

"It was fine, Papa," Amelia said, seeking to reassure her father and put an end to his worry. "Sir Benjamin was quite..." She fumbled for a word that would best describe her enigmatic, changeable host. "Agreeable."

"Agreeable, eh?" The admiral looked crestfallen. "What a pity. I was hoping for a bit of excitement around here with. Still, I suppose *agreeable* is a better trait in one's neighbours than any other. We must be grateful."

Silence reigned undisturbed once more and after a few moments more Amelia pushed her plate aside, her meal barely touched but feeling quite certain she could eat no more. The admiral ate heartily, for little on earth could interrupt that gentleman's appetite, and he seemed almost oblivious to Amelia's presence at the table beside him. She took to gazing out of the window, and it was this that led her to notice some movement, to squint, and to gasp in surprise at the less than welcome guest who appeared, at that moment, to be making his way towards their front door.

"What's that?" Admiral Sudbury asked, looking up from his meal and following Amelia's gaze to the window. "Mr Connelly! Jolly good, I had hoped he would come a-calling." He pushed himself back from the table, before glancing almost guiltily at his daughter. "That is, you do not mind him coming so early do you, Milly?"

"It is too late for me to mind it," Amelia remarked, as the sound of movement in the corridor suggested that their guest had crossed the threshold. She scooped up her book, feeling sure that the worthy curate would not approve of her reading Mrs Radcliffe, particularly not at the breakfast table, and had just managed to rearrange her features into an expression of sanguine calm as the door flew open and their guest was welcomed in.

"Good morning, Connelly!" Admiral Sudbury called, taking a swig of his rapidly cooling tea. "Come in and sit with us. You'll take a plate?"

"I have already eaten, Admiral." The curate demurred, then, noticing Amelia, he recovered himself and offered an altogether different opinion. "But I should not be averse to taking a cup of tea in the company of such good friends. And perhaps a morsel of bread?"

"Good man!" The Admiral handed his plate to a servant, summoning a fresh pot of tea and additional refreshments for their guest.

Amelia slid her book onto her lap, shielding it from Mr Connelly's eyes and, she hoped, his comments. He had once before had cause to lecture her on her choice of reading material and she did not feel quite equal to the task of receiving the lecture a second time so early in the day. She swallowed a yawn, but this, unfortunately, did not go unnoticed.

"I hope I am not calling on you too early, Miss Sudbury." Mr Connelly smiled, but the effect was so wide and exaggerated as to appear almost painful on the curate's thin face. "You know I am an early riser myself, and think it the very best course of action a Christian can undertake, to wake early and go about one's tasks while the *lazy man sleeps*."

"Aye, the admiralty would agree with you." Amelia's father chuckled. "I fear I could not stay in my bed half the morning, even if I wanted to. Years of activity on board ship has set me forever for waking early and retiring early. Ordinarily, Amelia has little choice but to wake early - nor should she choose otherwise. But we must allow her a little leeway today, Mr Connelly, for she was dining away from home last evening and therefore her normal routine was disrupted."

"Oh?" Mr Connelly turned his obsequious smile on Amelia for a second time, evidently angling for detail. She did not provide it, and the admiral took the opportunity to explain.

"She went to call at Roland Park and, trapped by the weather, was invited to stay and dine with them." He winked, heartily. "Although I have not yet been able to extract any worthwhile information regarding the new master of the house, unfortunately. All my Milly will say is that he is *agreeable*. Now, tell me, Curate, do you think she is truthful in this or is she keeping back some horror from father for fear of it upsetting me?"

"I would always have said that Miss Sudbury is entirely honest!" Mr Connelly said, with a loyalty Amelia was not sure she deserved. In fact, his hearty defence somewhat annoyed her. They were not well-acquainted, although their paths crossed a little more now that her father had sought to deepen his friendship. Even so, she could count on the fingers of one hand the notable exchanges she had shared with the young man beside her. What right had he to act as if he knew the inner workings of her mind? She opened her mouth to say as much, but the curate had begun to speak once more.

"I do hope that Sir Benjamin was a proper host, Miss Sudbury. I have not yet met him, myself, but one hears such stories -"

There was another flurry in the corridor, and both Amelia and the admiral exchanged confused looks until a low voice reached Amelia's ears, and she smiled, the first genuine expression that had rested on her features all morning.

"Mr Connelly, it seems you will be afforded the opportunity to judge the man for yourself. Father, it appears we are to be the social centre of Westham this morning."

The door opened, and Sir Benjamin Devereaux himself stood before them, clutching his hat to his chest, and wearing a smile that on any other man would have been tentative.

"Forgive the hour, Admiral Sudbury. We discovered this, after you had left, Miss Sudbury, and my sister did not like to think of your being without it. I took it upon myself to see it was returned to you."

He passed her the reticule she had carried with her all day and not even realised was no longer in her possession, and as he did so their fingers brushed. Amelia let go the reticule too soon and it would have dropped to the ground, had Sir Benjamin's grip not held fast. He set it down on the table and was poised to bid the party farewell when the admiral stood.

"Well, you must not lurk in the doorway, Sir Benjamin. Come in and be seated, do. I have just sent for more tea. You'll take a cup? Excellent. Have you met our curate, Mr Connelly...?"

⁂

DEVEREAUX FOLDED HIMSELF, with difficulty, into a spare seat around the dining table. He had not been expecting to be invited to join the family, although he could not own to regretting the invitation. He had only ridden over so early so as to assure himself of Amelia's being there but now that he had seen her again he wondered if he had made a mistake. She would not look at him but kept her eyes fixed on the table before her. It was her father who rose to the challenge of playing host, and a more jovial man Sir Benjamin had not met in all of Westham. *Not that I have been looking*, he thought. Still, he could not help but like Amelia's father. He had the same forthright attitude as his daughter, he laughed loudly and often and made sitting around that particular table at that particular hour a pleasant occupation.

"You will join us for the service on Sunday, I hope?"

Ben turned, surprised to hear the Sudburys' other guest speak, at last, when he had thus far been silent, shooting Ben the sort of looks he had grown to expect from new acquaintances in Westham.

"That is what one does on a Sunday, is not it?" Ben's smart answer was out almost before he was aware of having thought it and although he won a scowl from the clergyman he thought he detected a sparkle of merriment in the admiral's eyes.

"It is what most *civilised members* of society do on a Sunday," the curate muttered, his unspoken inference being, of course, that Devereaux was not to be counted amongst them.

"If the church is only opened to the most civilised, sir, I wager your pews are more often empty than they are full." Ben smiled, as sweetly as he could, to indicate that he meant his words in jest, however genuinely he might also feel them. Amelia had lifted her eyes to him at this exchange, and they widened as if she was not sure whether to laugh or scold him. She did neither, hurrying to change the subject, though whether this was for his sake or the clergyman's, he was not sure.

"I hope you received Papa's letter, Mr Connelly. I tried to deliver it whilst running errands yesterday but alas! You were not at home, nor at the church." She smiled, ruefully. "It was a day of disappointments for me, for I left home with a list of tasks to accomplish and achieved not one of them."

The curate's features shifted, abruptly and completely. He shot a superior glance at Devereaux before turning a simpering smile on Miss Sudbury.

"Indeed, Miss Sudbury, I was quite disconsolate to have missed you! I stepped out to run a few errands of my own. What a pity our paths did not cross!"

He let out a snivelling laugh that was intended, Ben supposed, to be endearing, and to promote inquiry but as nobody asked any further question of him he allowed the laugh to die away before continuing on, unprompted, his voice taking on the timbre of a sermon, though his pulpit was but a seat at another man's breakfast table.

"A curate's time, I feel, is never truly his own, you see. There are always a great many tasks to be completed, parishioners to call upon, studies to adhere to, and many hours of solitary contemplation of the words of our great teacher." He paused, before adding, unnecessarily, that teacher's name. "Jesus."

Ben nodded with interest as if he had never before heard mention of this particular messiah, and Amelia, catching his eye, struggled to swallow a laugh.

"I know *you*, Miss Sudbury, understand and share my great compassion for the poor. It is our responsibility, as civilised, Christian men - and women, of course, haha! - to devote to these poor, miserable wretches our time and our pity, as the Lord would have us do."

"Mr Connelly," Ben said, tiring of the lecture though it had scarcely begun. "Do you seek to *help* these miserable wretches on whom you lavish your time and pity? In a practical manner?"

Mr Connelly's pious smile faltered.

"What do you mean, Sir Benjamin?"

"Well, if you see a man without work, do you make it your business to find him some? If a family is starving, do you provide them with food from your own kitchen?"

"I - I am a bachelor and scarcely have means of providing a hearty meal for myself. No, I, too, rely on charity -"

"Which you do not then share with those less fortunate than yourself?" Ben was baiting the man, then, but he did not care. He had little patience with those who made claims to piety and yet made no practical action to alleviate the suffering of those around them.

"Do you?"

Amelia's crisp, musical voice rang like a bell, bringing all the men to attention. She was looking directly at Ben, at last, but instead of enjoying the victory of having won her attention to himself, Ben felt her challenge and was determined to meet it well.

"I am the master of an estate, Miss Sudbury. I have little choice but to take interest in the lives of my tenants. If I hear of them suffering, I do what I can to help them. Not to win rewards in heaven. God has seen fit to position me thus, I am sure he expects no less of me than to do my duty."

"How interesting you speak of duty, Sir Benjamin, where I speak of charity -"

"Are they not one and the same?"

"Gentlemen!" Admiral Sudbury set down his teacup and laughed, merrily bringing the discussion to a close before it could grow any more heated. "I fear we are straying into territory far too learned for the breakfast table." His eyes sought out Amelia's. "We shall have to invite Sir Benjamin to dine here one night, Milly, shall we not? Then we shall be guaranteed of some good conversation." He turned back to Devereaux, beaming with delight at what he evidently thought was a very good idea. "My daughter can give quite as good as she gets, Sir Benjamin, when it comes to discussions of moral philosophy and religion. Quite outfoxes poor Mr Connelly here, doesn't she, Samuel?"

The curate turned a peculiar shade of purple and stammered a rebuttal, but Ben scarcely noticed. His eyes strayed once more to Amelia, and he found his interest rising yet again in this enigma of a young lady.

"If you would be kind enough to invite me, Admiral Sudbury, I would be only too eager to dine with you," he said, fixing a warm, knowing smile on Amelia. She kept her gaze averted but colour seeped into her cheeks and Ben, noting the power he had on her, merely smiled all the wider. "I shall bring both my opinions and my wits, for I am sure I shall need both if I am to defend myself against your daughter."

Chapter Nine

Amelia could only sigh with relief when breakfast, at last, reached its conclusion. The meal had lasted twice its usual length, for neither of their two callers seemed eager to leave and it was the admiral, at last, who compelled the meal to end by declaring his intention to take a walk. Ordinarily, Amelia would accompany him, but Mr Connelly had been so quick to offer his services that Amelia had demurred, claiming that she would prefer to spend the day indoors catching up on her reading.

"I ought to take my leave, also," Sir Benjamin said, striding towards the door. "I have already taken up more of your time than I intended, and poor Miss Sudbury will soon tire of me if our paths persist in crossing so frequently."

This comment was made innocently enough, but she was already of the opinion that there was nothing *innocent* about Sir Benjamin Devereaux. The smile he shot her as he said this was proof enough of that. She flinched and her book, which had been sitting, forgotten, on her lap, fell to the ground with a thump.

"Dear me, what was that?" the admiral exclaimed, as Amelia bent down to retrieve it. Devereaux was quicker, again displaying the accursed quick reflexes that had betrayed him the previous evening. The reminder of how her conversation with Joanna had been overheard and likely ruminated on and mused over at leisure by the very man it had at least partly concerned made Amelia blush. The heat in her cheeks intensified as he laid the book down on the table but not before flipping it open and scanning the title page with eyes that widened almost imperceptibly.

"A romance?" he mused aloud. "And here, Admiral Sudbury led me to believe that his daughter only sought to occupy her mind with titles that promoted moral virtue, philosophical betterment and compassion for one's fellow man."

"And you think novels do not do this?" Amelia blurted out her response, snatching up the book and hugging it to her chest as if it were a shield.

"Now, Miss Sudbury, you surely cannot mean to argue that the works of Mrs Radcliffe are of equivalent worth and value as a collection of sermons?" Mr Connelly chuckled, the simpering high-pitched laugh he seemed to reserve for in her presence alone, and which served to rile her nerves most intently. "Oh, I dare say they are entertaining for a young lady as unworldly as yourself -"

"Am I unworldly?" Amelia asked. The expressions that flitted across first her father's and then Sir Benjamin's features suggested that this was indeed the case, and in one man's opinion at least that was all for the better. Poor Mr Connelly seemed not to know how best to answer her question without causing offence to one of his hosts, and instead took a great interest in the clock.

"Dear me, the time! Admiral Sudbury, I must apologise most profusely, for I have just remembered a certain appointment I have outstanding with a parishioner..."

His gaze settled on the third gentleman present.

"Perhaps, Sir Benjamin, you would care to accompany me?"

"Do you need an escort?" Devereaux asked, in a vaguely mocking tone. Straightening and glancing at the admiral, he appeared to repent of the action, for he nodded his head and agreed that he would quite contentedly accompany the curate into town, provided Admiral Sudbury did not mind him leaving his horse in their stable a while longer.

"I shall retrieve it on my return," he promised.

"Good man!" Admiral Sudbury said. "And you'll stop in for a moment when you do, I hope? We have scarcely had a chance to get acquainted and I do feel a gentleman's friendship grows best over a chess board." He smiled, hopefully. "Do you play?"

"Do I play!" Devereaux laughed, but it was not the simpering, ingratiating sound that so often tripped from the curate's lips, nor the cruel, mocking tone that Devereaux himself had deployed against his stepmother the previous evening. This was a pleasant sound and a genuine one, so warmly endearing that Amelia could not help but look up at him. He seemed both like and unlike the gentleman she had met the previous day and she found herself captivated by the light and shadows as they played across his handsome features.

"In that case, we shall try a game this afternoon," the admiral said, with a decided nod. "Battle shall commence at precisely one o'clock."

"Aye, captain," Devereaux said, with a bow, before straightening enough that he could quirk an eyebrow in their general direction. "Or rather, aye *Admiral*."

"Well, good-day, Admiral Sudbury," Mr Connelly said, struggling to maintain a neutral expression. He certainly did not seem to have warmed to Sir Benjamin Devereaux on this first meeting. Amelia was surprised to find that this fact, far from reminding her of her own stilted first impressions of the man before her actually served to raise him in her estimations. She had made no pretence of fondness towards either gentleman, yet had she to choose between the two, Devereaux was looking dangerously close to the one she would prefer. This thought startled her and she stood, hurrying to open the door to the gentlemen and relieved when they had both departed, leaving her alone with her father. The breakfast room felt strangely empty without their guests and too large, which was not often a thought Amelia had concerning the small, sunny room.

"Well, my dear! That was an eventful breakfast," Admiral Sudbury said, standing and looking about him for the cane he took with him on his daily walk. "I am glad to have seen both gentlemen, although I wager it was not me they hastened over here to see."

"Oh?" Amelia squeaked, praying the heat she felt flood into her cheeks was not quite as evident to her father as she felt it must be.

"You need not worry, pet, I shan't speak of it anymore." His eyes twinkled. "I shall leave you to your worldly literature, saints preserve us, and attend to my walk."

Amelia smiled, bidding her father good morning, and eventually found her page again as he closed the door behind him. Although her eyes rested on a particularly interesting snippet of dialogue she did not read a word of it. Her mind was too busy replaying the conversation that had taken place around this very dining table, and wondering how it could be that the man she had been certain was the villain in her own pastoral drama seemed to be changing before her very eyes into something almost heroic.

DEVEREAUX WAS ONLY too pleased to bid farewell to his walking companion as they drew within sight of the home at which the curate was due to visit. They had walked in stony silence for the duration of their journey, for Ben had little interest in small-talk, and the curate seemed incapable of speaking to him at all. As they slowed to part, Ben turned to bid the man a farewell, wondering if he ought to have made more of an effort to win the young man to his side. Although he had sensed in the Sudburys' dining room that the curate did not approve of him, he might have shown him another side. He might have been the wealthy, generous Benjamin Devereaux who won friends wherever he went. He grimaced. He did not suppose this particular gentleman's good opinion would be secured so easily. Surely a man who had devoted his energies to the furtherance of the heavenly kingdom had little enough interest in a gentleman's purse, however weighty it turned out to be.

"Good day Mr Connelly," he said, rearranging his features into a vaguely friendly smile. "I am glad to have made your acquaintance." It was not an outright lie. If he was to make his home in Roland Park he would have cause to know his neighbours, after all. "Perhaps I will see you on Sunday."

The curate raised his eyes momentarily before struggling to wrangle his features into polite disinterest.

"You will be very welcome," he said, in a voice that suggested this was not quite the truth. "Forgive me, I ought to have enquired before now, how is your poor mother?"

Ben's eyes glazed over.

"My mother has been at rest this past fifteen years. I assume you refer to the Lady Devereaux who is still living? My stepmother."

"Ah! Erm...yes." The curate coloured, and Ben felt a flare of guilt at making the poor man so uncomfortable. He strove to inject some warmth into his voice.

"She rallies, I believe."

"I hope she was not brought too low by grief."

Ben struggled to restrain a smile. No, indeed, it was not grief that brought poor Lady Devereaux low, but fear of what the future held.

"I believe it was you, Mr Connelly, who wrote to me on the occasion of my father's death." He held out a hand. "For that, I must thank you. Without your letter, I am not sure quite when I would have heard and it is far better to receive such news in the privacy of one's own rooms than by the surprise arrival of a solicitor. Thank you."

A little taken aback by this warm and genuine gratitude, it took the curate a few moments to find his tongue in order to offer a response. He shook Ben's hand limply at first but then with a little more energy.

"Of course. I supposed your mother - ah - Lady Devereaux - had already written to you herself, but I always think it incumbent on the local minister to write personally when a family has experienced such a loss." He made an awkward, rasping laugh. "I did not dare to imagine my little note would summon you here, yet how grateful your family must be to have you amongst them once more. Well, Sir Benjamin, I shall - I shall look forward to seeing you on Sunday." His smile bordered on sycophantic. "I trust you will enjoy our small chapel, although I dare say it cannot compare to the grandeur of the churches you visited in London."

Ben smiled, not daring to disillusion the poor man by admitting he rarely had cause to set foot inside of a church in London and associated most often with folks who were even less inclined to moral self-improvement than he. Bidding him farewell, he resumed his walk, determining he would explore the small town a little before returning to see the Sudburys and collect his horse. Although their plans were not set for some time yet he felt quite confident that his new friend would not begrudge him an earlier arrival.

A smile tugged at his lips. He would also not be disappointed to see Amelia again. He shook his head, amused at his own ridiculousness. Were he listening to a friend of his speak so warmly of a young lady he had been acquainted with a little less than twenty-four hours, he would be scathing indeed. Add to that the knowledge that this particular young lady was a close personal friend of the sister who despised him and the situation seemed utterly hopeless. She was not remarkable nor wealthy nor titled and yet somehow that seemed to distinguish Miss Amelia Sudbury from all others. When she spoke, it was without the guile and calculation of London's society misses and whilst her eyes flared with fire when she considered his rumoured misdeeds, there was something else there that she could not quite hide from his scrutiny: she was intrigued by him. Perhaps she sought some real-life experience to rival her novels. He rolled his eyes skywards. No doubt she thought him a villain. Did that, then, make the curate her hero? The thought was amusing, and Ben's smile widened. That any young lady could find the curate preferable to him struck him as nonsense until he recalled the way his own sister had spoken of him, in Amelia's hearing, whilst she though him sleeping. *Mary.* She had mentioned Miss Bell, which suggested she *knew* about Miss Bell or knew whatever version of events her mother had told her. His smile became a scowl. No doubt Amelia knew it too and it was this that would keep her from ever caring to know him better. *She does not know me at all,* he fumed. *And if my sister continues to poison her against me, she never will!*

The thought ought not to have bothered him. He had known of her existence little more than a day and surely there were twenty others like her even in this small town. If it was a change from London society he pined for, he had found it, and surely these ladies were all equally interchangeable. He sighed. That was not true and he knew it. Even if he did chance to meet a dozen other ladies as intriguing to him as Miss Amelia Sudbury, they would still not care to know *him* on account of his rakish reputation. That reputation was useful to him in London, for it weeded out those who would use proximity to him for their own ends. He had not fully considered how much more of a hindrance it would be upon returning home.

He turned back, retracing the steps he had so recently walked in the company of the curate. Perhaps it would serve him well to cultivate a friendship with the young minister. It might help to counter the worst of the lies his stepmother had spread concerning him.

He would meet the town en massed at the upcoming assembly. Did he really have time to change his reputation before then? He might lay the groundwork at least. Yes, and he had begun it already. His mood lifted as he walked back towards the house, all of a sudden eager to spend a little time with the admiral again. His near neighbour would surely help him, for he had seemed genuinely pleased to make Ben's acquaintance. With a welcome from an admiral of the navy and the beginnings of a friendship with the local curate, perhaps Benjamin might begin at last to shed his rakish reputation for a better one.

Chapter Ten

Devereaux was as good as his word. At one o'clock sharp, he was admitted to Admiral Sudbury's study and the heavy oak door closed behind him.

Amelia, lurking on the turn of the stairs, observed his arrival without herself being observed or so she thought. Benjamin turned to close the door and as he did his eyes lifted up the staircase towards her. Too late to move, he noticed her and, she thought, his smile broadened momentarily. But perhaps she imagined this. What she did not imagine was the wink he directed towards her, and she was so startled that she almost tripped on the stair and tumbled down after him.

Furious at his ability to discompose her with one glance, she turned on her heel and marched upwards, hoping and equally dreading that the sound would carry to her father's study and alert the gentlemen to the true state of her mood. The fearful notion that, out of concern, her father might send a servant to enquire after her health or come himself was enough to return Amelia to her senses, and when she closed her door she did it gently, tiptoeing across the length of her small bedroom to the window. She had fashioned for herself a seat from the wide windowsill, festooned with cushions and blankets which rendered it a cosy seat even on the coldest winter days. Here she sat and read, crossing time and distance and becoming a hundred different people in the space of hours.

Today, when she tried to read, she found herself distracted. It was just like at breakfast time, and once again she could lay the blame for her inattention firmly at the expensive leather-booted feet of Sir Benjamin Devereaux.

She bit her lip. Even the sound of his name was enough to quicken her heart-rate, and she laid a hand over her breast as if to urge it to slow. She was angry at its lack of co-operation, for it seemed that, no matter what reasons her mind might give to compel her heart to disregard Sir Benjamin, her foolish heart paid no attention and would fix its affections wherever it chose. *However unlikely, inopportune, unfortunate and idiotic!*

Laying her book aside, she turned her attention to the window itself. She had always liked this view, which overlooked their garden to the edge of her home and beyond that to Roland Park. She scowled. There, again, was Sir Benjamin, disturbing her peace and inserting himself into her mind at every opportunity.

Her eyes turned to the door, and she wondered how the gentlemen's chess game was proceeding. She was glad her father had found a new opponent, for there were few in Westham who could pose any sort of challenge to the admiral when it came to chess. His own skill and strategy had been honed on the battlefield before it was ever practised on the chess-board, and as such he was a worthy opponent to any who might seek to play him. The ghost of a smile tugged at Amelia's lips. At least Sir Benjamin had confidence. Whether he had the skill to match it would remain to be seen, but she felt it likely that he did and would offer her father at least a modest challenge.

Wrenching her attention back, she tried to focus on something else. Anything else! How could it be that she had met Sir Benjamin Devereaux only one day previously and already he had found his way into the fabric of her thoughts? She had met people before, although it had been quite some time since there had been so talked-about a new arrival in Westham. In fact, the most recent arrivals had probably been her own family, when the admiral had secured their home and settled them there. Her brother had been but a fleeting companion, for Arthur was as often away at sea as he were at home, and when he was in Westham he caused a stir all his own. Amelia smiled, recalling more than one young lady who had lost her heart to a potential Sudbury suitor. He had left without any exchange of promise, though, and Amelia had found herself with several friends in the immediate interim, all young ladies angling for news of the handsome sailor. Time had passed and interest had waned, and the young ladies who had once pledged themselves unlikely to ever meet another man so dashing, so handsome, so charming as the young Arthur Sudbury had found other gentlemen less likely to uproot and head for the sea. They were happy. Amelia frowned. She had not approved of her brother toying with young ladies affections that way, although he claimed there was nothing dishonourable in his behaviour. Papa had taken Arthur's side, of course, laughing and agreeing that the poor fellow could hardly help it if young ladies fell in love with him. That was the curse of being so handsome and amiable a young man and facing the promise of a successful naval career. Amelia had rolled her eyes then and did so again now, but the recollection had re-ordered her thoughts into an entirely different direction. With a less sympathetic teller, the story could paint her brother in a much darker light. Arthur could be thought careless, even cruel, with other people's hearts. Was it possible that there were the same two sides to Sir Benjamin Devereaux?

No. He had embarked upon an affair with a governess - a woman of unequal status and in his father's employ. And where was that poor young lady now? Cast aside, no doubt, in order for him to continue his womanising, drinking and general bad behaviour in London. Amelia hardened her heart against him or tried to. Were not the seducers and scoundrels of the novels she loved to read also often blessed with a charming nature? It did not follow that he, like her brother, had an honourable heart underneath it all. He may not have a heart at all! She had learnt of Devereaux's true nature from his own sister. Who else could know the man better?

"I will not lose *my* heart to him," she promised, even as the offending muscle began once again to beat a staccato at the mere image her mind conjured up. His smile, widened as it turned on her, the wink she was now certain she could not have imagined as he closed the door to her father's study. Let him befriend her father if he would. He would be their neighbour. Even if he were not Joanna's brother, she would be forced into an acquaintance with him and she was able to act as agreeably as such an association demanded. But that was all. She would not allow herself to fall any further under his spell.

ADMIRAL SUDBURY'S WATERY eyes scanned the chessboard, his hand hovering first one way, then the other. At last, a sly smile tugging his weather-beating lips into a smile, he snatched up a piece and set it down again with a flourish.

"Checkmate." He folded his hands in satisfaction, nestling them under his chin, and eyed Devereaux with delight. "I think, sir, that the victory is mine."

"Well won and well deserved," Ben said, with a concessionary smile. He leaned back in his seat, chuckling. "It is a long time since I have played such a challenging game."

"The same is true for me!" Admiral Sudbury gathered his pieces. "I do not suppose I can persuade you to play again?"

"Perhaps in a little while..." Ben conceded, stifling a yawn with the back of his hand. It was no exaggeration to declare his wits fully exercised by the game they had just concluded. He would require a little respite before waging a second campaign.

"Perhaps after some refreshments?" The admiral waggled his bushy grey eyebrows and reached down, opening a drawer in the bureau behind him and retrieving a bottle of not-unrespectable brandy. "Come, Devereaux. You will not leave me to drink alone, I hope?"

Ben grinned, never one to refuse hospitality when it was offered to him. He took the glass his host passed him with a grateful nod.

"There, now! That's two reasons to rejoice at your coming to Westham," Admiral Sudbury remarked, taking a sip and leaning back in his own chair with a contented sigh. "You are a fair opponent at chess. More than fair, in fact, for I won that game by luck rather than by skill. I wager our next match will have a different outcome." His eyes sparkled. "I have been limited in my playing of late. Mr Connelly tries, but he is pedestrian at best." His smile became a grimace. "And sober as a judge, without your good humour."

The picture Admiral Sudbury conjured of the serious, sensible curate was so accurate to the man Ben had met that morning that he could not help but roar with laughter. He slapped his hand against his chest.

"I see I must watch myself around you or risk receiving just such an unflinching assessment of my own shortcomings." He took a sip of his brandy, relishing the warmth as it made its way down his throat. "Of which, I assure you, there are many."

Admiral Sudbury fixed him with a look that was not easily shaken off, but when he spoke his voice was light and Ben relaxed.

"I do not doubt there are always many words shared about newcomers to as small a town as this." He grimaced. "I dare not think what was said of my own family when we arrived."

"How long have you lived here?" It seemed unlikely to Ben that Westham had existed without the admiral's steadying presence, yet he knew their family must have arrived sometime during his absence, for he had no earlier memory of the near neighbours.

"Almost ten years," the admiral said, his gaze resting briefly on two miniatures that lay, propped up, on the mantel. One, a woman, was unmistakably like Amelia, although lacking her easy smile and determined chin.

"My wife," Admiral Sudbury explained. "Died five years ago this past Spring." He raised his glass in silent salute to the absent Mrs Sudbury. "A finer lady I have never met....although my Milly is becoming more like her with every day that passes." He grinned. "I dare say you will call me sentimental to hold such an opinion and you'd be right." He took a hearty sip of his drink, and Ben's eyes turned once more to the miniatures.

"And the other?" he asked when there had been a moment of silence between the two gentlemen.

"My son," Admiral Sudbury said. "Arthur. He's in the Indies at present. A captain."

Ben's eyebrows raised in spite of himself. He wondered what this male version of Amelia might be like. He had worked hard to advance, surely, and was deserving of the evident pride his father took in him. Ben felt a pang of regret that his own father would never have had cause to speak of him in so warm and tender a manner and, fearing his features might betray the dark turn his thoughts had taken, he took a hasty sip of his drink.

"I dare say it is not fashionable to speak with such evident affection of one's offspring," the admiral said, without a trace of embarrassment. "You will find that being here, amidst country folk, one may be rather less concerned with what is *fashionable.*" His lips pursed as he said the word, as if the notion itself left a bad taste in his mouth. A moment later and his self-deprecating smile was back in place. "And I'm sure my daughter would be mortified to hear me speak so. She has great aspirations, Sir Benjamin, although I fear she is somewhat encouraged in her thinking by your sister." He leant forward, with interest. "I hope you are not struggling too much in a household filled with ladies?"

This was asked so innocently that Ben could do nought but laugh, again. On the lips of any other man - any other person, in fact! - this would be incorrigible fishing for information. On the lips of the admiral, though, it could be taken for nothing but genuine concern. He, who had been so often amongst men, so regularly in pursuit of male accomplishments and interests, must surely rail at the notion of occupying a house of women. Certain of Benjamin's friends would not feel the burden half so heavy and the thought crossed his mind, unbidden, of what George Lenox would make of his situation. He struggled to maintain his composure.

"I assure you, Admiral, that a household of but two women is not quite the trial you imagine..." He trailed off, fearing that, if he spoke longer, he would confess to it not being the number but the nature of these particular ladies that caused him a problem.

"Well, it shall do us both good to have another gentleman nearby, I do not doubt!" the admiral declared, draining the remnants of his glass and turning his attention back to the chess board. "Now, Sir Benjamin. Might I tempt you with a second match? Or have I taken too much of your time already?"

Chapter Eleven

B enjamin Devereaux became such a regular visitor that Amelia had developed numerous ways to avoid him whenever he appeared. It seemed to her that she became entirely unlike herself whenever they were forced into company and she did not like the way he seemed to know just what she was thinking even without her saying a word. There was another reason she was eager to hide when Sir Benjamin Devereaux was nearby – she had not yet mentioned his invitation to her to accompany their party to Malton. Her father would not mind. He was generous to his daughter and it was less an ability to afford a new dress than it was a complete lack of realisation that Amelia might want one that had prevented him from making the suggestion himself. No, if Admiral Sudbury heard that a party from Roland Park intended to visit the nearby town of Malton for shopping, he would insist upon Amelia accompanying them and likely come along himself, for he was not immune to the pull of the local town, the hustle and bustle of the crowds and the opportunity to reconnect with old friends. There was scarcely a town in all of England where the admiral did not have some acquaintance or other he was eager to see again. Yet still, Amelia hesitated to mention the promised trip for reasons she could not entirely understand herself.

That particular afternoon Sir Benjamin was not expected. Indeed, he had called on the admiral only one day previously, so it was considered entirely *un*likely that he would call a second time. Amelia was curled up quite contentedly in the parlour poring over a book. Her enjoyment of reading had returned to her with her avoidance of Benjamin Devereaux and she was so caught up in a particularly compelling adventure that she did not hear the ringing of the bell, nor notice the commotion as their guest was shown into the parlour. She had been vaguely aware of her father leaving the room, momentarily, hunting after some letter he had laid down and now wished to consult so when the door opened she half-expected it to be his return, clutching the wayward paper.

"Did you find it?" she mused, not looking up from a thrilling account of a highwayman's pursuit of the heroic Lord Eldred.

"Find what?" a deep, throaty voice, loaded with humour, asked.

Amelia darted up, instantly regretting the way she had lolled on the sofa as if she were a child and not a grown woman of almost twenty.

"Oh!" she cried, smoothing down her skirts, and turning her pages as she did so.

"Miss Sudbury!" Sir Benjamin exclaimed, with an amused, ironical grin. "I fear you have never come across a most excellent technological advancement - a bookmark." He patted his chest, before squirrelling one hand inside his greatcoat, returning with a prize - a strip of leather inlaid with gold. "This is the second time at least I have come upon you and noticed you lose your place." He arched an eyebrow. "Or, perhaps, I have caused you to lose it."

Amelia flushed hotly and was just summoning the courage to mutter a refutation of his claim, when he, noticing her discomfort waved her anger away with a slight tremor of his fingers.

"Ah, I ought not to speak so freely to the daughter of my friend, I know." He bowed, contritely, and continued to hold out the bookmark to her. "Take it, do, and may it help you make better progress in your reading." He straightened. "I came to see your father and was given to believe he was here with you. Ought I to go away again?"

"N-no," Amelia said, with a wary smile. "He stepped out but a moment, although -"

"Devereaux!" Admiral Sudbury croaked. "I thought I heard you. What good timing you have, for I was just setting down to attend to my correspondence, a task I deplore and am always eager to escape. You'll stop for tea, won't you? Oh, Amelia, you're still here. Wonderful! Poor Sir Benjamin was beginning to develop quite a complex that whenever he should chance to appear, you chose to disappear. I tried to tell him it was nothing personal, and yet..."

Her father continued to talk, utterly oblivious to the effect his words were having on at least one of the two young people present. Benjamin Devereaux blushed - indeed, Amelia could almost not credit it as truth at first, and a second surreptitious glance was required to confirm that a deep red tinge dotted their guest's high cheekbones, although his features remained impassive. No, not quite impassive. She saw the merest hint of a smile tug at his lips, but it was not quite the same smug smile he had a tendency to wear during their exchanges - of which she could count but three and had memorized every breath, every blink that passed between them. This smile was humble and self-deprecating, and she liked it all the more.

"Shall I - shall I request some tea?" she blurted, eager to spare Sir Benjamin his blushes and to escape the truth that her father skirted - for it was not a lie that she sought to hide whenever Sir Benjamin was near. She had not thought him aware of it, though, and now discovering that he had been, she felt a little ashamed of her behaviour. "I will come right back," she promised, glancing from her father to Sir Benjamin and risking a tentative smile. His eyes met hers, and she found it took rather more effort than she would have imagined to wrench her gaze away.

"Very good." Admiral Sudbury beamed, and made his way back to his seat, discarding his hard-found letter at random as he passed an end-table. "Come, come, Ben. Have a seat. You have not walked all this way, have you?"

"You say *all this way* as if there were more than a mere mile distance separating our properties, Admiral," Benjamin remarked, with a droll smile. He claimed an empty chair as his own. "And as if I am not greatly benefitted by the taking of such exercise."

"Ha!" Admiral Sudbury barked, but he was delighted by this good-natured teasing and strove to give back as good as he had received. "Had I the energy to return the favour, I assure you I would." His eyes twinkled. "At least, I would consider it. I wager the feminine half of my household is a mite more hospitable than your own, though, eh, Devereaux?"

Amelia wished she could linger to overhear Sir Benjamin's response to this. Whether she would prefer to hear herself praised or her friend slighted she was not sure. Alas, she could do neither without her intent to eavesdrop being fully evident to both gentlemen. She took her leave, but was somewhat slow in moving away from the door, so that Sir Benjamin's warm voice be discernible as long as possible.

⚜

DEVEREAUX HAD BEEN a little cautious of coming to call again on Admiral and Miss Sudbury. Politeness dictated he ought not to be so often amongst his neighbours as to make himself unwelcome, but he found he was unable to stay away from there for long. He craved the company of the admiral, the first and best friend he had made since leaving London, and, if he were honest with himself, he longed to see Amelia again. He swallowed. The admiral had not been wrong in recounting their conversation, although Ben rather wished Amelia had not been there to hear it. It made him appear weak. Worse, it confessed that she was often a topic of conversation between the two gentlemen. Yet she had not seemed to mind, nor really to notice the implication of such an admission on her father's part. Ben sighed. She had also not stirred herself to deny her father's assertions, to summon some excuse to explain that her absences whenever Ben set foot in their home were mere coincidence and not an attempt to avoid a gentleman she did not wish to see.

This pained him more than he cared to admit. It angered him that anybody would shun him without knowing him, although he had come, during the last few days, to expect such treatment. Everyone seemed to know of his past misdeeds, or the rumours surrounding him. No doubt his stepmother had seen to that but even if she had not, rumours took on a life of their own and the sudden disappearance of the young Benjamin Devereaux would have been conjured its own explanation. That the young gentlemen had remained absent this past ten years, never even returning to the home he had grown up in for holidays was likewise suspicious and must have given some truth to the stories. He lived with them, now, and was very much aware of the curious stares that greeted him in town, the parents who edged a little closer to him so that their daughters would not. The conversations that were drawn hastily to a close before they even really began.

I do not care, he told himself, holding his head high and refusing to demonstrate any kind of reaction. *What does it matter to me if provincial people judge me on stories I know to be untrue?*

But he did care. He cared that he was judged so swiftly and completely. He cared that the stories that were nursed as truth had but a germ of reality to them and he was afforded no chance to clear his name.

Not so for the admiral. If his friend had heard the stories, he made no reference to them, but greeted Ben as a welcome addition to their small hamlet, grateful to have a neighbour he could also consider a friend.

The door opened, and Amelia returned, slipping noiselessly into a seat opposite her father.

"The tea will come shortly," she murmured.

Devereaux smiled his thanks at her, before turning his attention back to his host, realising, to his shame, that whilst he had been lost in thought Admiral Sudbury had been speaking and he had not heard a word.

"Forgive me, Admiral, you were saying?" He shifted in his seat, uncrossing his long legs and leaning forward a little so as to better hear his friend.

"I doubt it would be of interest to you, Devereaux!" the admiral declared, with a self-deprecating smile. "I was merely waxing lyrical about my time in the navy, and forgot it was you and not my ship-mad son sitting opposite me."

This provoked a musical laugh from Amelia, and Ben turned towards her, eager to continue the joke if it would encourage her to remain in the room with them.

"I wonder, Miss Sudbury, if I ought to take that for a compliment, or not?" he arched an eyebrow. "What say you, am I like your brother at all?"

Amelia's laugh died away, and a flash of colour darted across her cheeks. Ben wondered if he had spoken too freely and replayed his words in his mind, seeking what might have caused the young lady before him any offence. He was so used to the ladies he met in London, who he sometimes sought intentionally to offend if only to buy himself some respite from their suffocating company. He was always adept at winning their good opinion when he wanted it but not, it seemed, in Westham. He cleared his throat, casting about for some change in topic that might negate the deathly silence when Amelia's quiet voice spoke again.

"I fear, Sir Benjamin, you would not think it a compliment if you knew my brother. *Ship-mad* is politeness: I do not believe him capable of uttering a word not relating in some manner to the sea."

Admiral Sudbury laughed.

"Tis true, I bred another just like me." He glanced up as the door opened once more, and rubbed his hands in delight at the arrival of their promised refreshments. "Amelia is more like her mother, God rest her soul, and so balances Arthur and I quite well."

"He has been away a long time?" Benjamin asked, accepting the cup of tea that was offered to him, and directing his question to the room at large, although secretly hoping Amelia might be the one to answer it. His hopes must have been heard, for she nodded, and began once more to speak.

"He is in the Indies at present, as I am sure Father has already told you. But before that, he spent some time in Africa. He was in Ireland, and we were fortunate to visit him there."

Colour deepened in her cheeks momentarily, and Ben correctly deduced this was warmth at a pleasant memory, and not embarrassment or anger. He seized upon it, fixing his attention directly on her and urging her to continue.

"Ireland! I have never been there, myself, although I have a friend who has travelled there extensively. Tell me, is it as beautiful as I have heard, or has Lennox misled me?"

"Oh, it is lovely," Amelia said, setting down her tea so that she could better describe the mountains and the trees, using her hands to illustrate an image in the air in front of her. He nodded, surprised and pleased to see her so animated in her explanation and enchanted with the picture she conjured up of vast green spaces, hills and wild places.

"I see, now, where your mind returns to when you read," he said, with a nod towards her book, forgotten on the sofa beside her. "You escape back to Ireland, forsaking dreary society and small-town manners for the wilds of the natural world." His smile grew. "You wish to read of adventures, knights and villains, yet I wager you would not enjoy living amongst them."

Amelia's smile froze.

"I am sure you would know more about that than I, Sir Benjamin." She reached for her tea and made a great show of stirring it, with such vehemence that it spilt over the side and pooled in its saucer. Feeling himself quite thoroughly dismissed, Ben turned back to the admiral, who had been watching this exchange with an expression of interest in his pale grey eyes.

"Has Miss Sudbury told you of our own plans for travelling this coming Tuesday?" Ben asked, taking a sip of his tea to punctuate his words. Amelia's teaspoon clinked against the side of her cup, and Ben looked at her in surprise. She was biting down on her lip and he realised, all at once, that she had evidently *not* mentioned their plans to her father. He wondered why not but before he could puzzle out an answer the admiral had asked him a question.

"Travel plans?" The ghost of a smile settled on his weathered face. "Do not tell me you plan to go as far as Ireland, Sir Benjamin?"

"No, indeed!" Ben laughed, shortly. "Merely Malton. My sister wishes to purchase a new dress and invited Amelia, as her closest companion, to accompany us." He paused, feeling Amelia's eyes on him. "You are most welcome to come with us as well, Admiral, should you wish to."

"Malton?" Admiral Sudbury meditated on the suggestion, drinking deeply of his own teacup before responding. "Why, I have not been there in close to a year. And to buy a dress?"

he looked, askance, at his daughter. "You did not mention the need of one, Amelia. For the assembly, I suppose." He shook his head. "I shall never understand the whims of young ladies. But, if Miss Devereaux is to have a new dress I dare say Miss Sudbury might care for one too." He smiled merrily at his daughter. "I shall happily oblige, and happily accompany you if you have room in your carriage?"

"Indeed, plenty," Ben promised, cheered by Admiral Sudbury's words and the promise of another gentleman's presence in their party. Perhaps Amelia might relax if her father was present and he, Devereaux, would not feel so outnumbered by ladies if he had a friend of his own alongside them.

Chapter Twelve

"Is that Devereaux's carriage, Milly?"

Admiral Sudbury had been making inquiries of this nature to his daughter at ten-minute intervals all morning but instead of finding them an irritation, Amelia was encouraged and amused by her father's excitement. He had the appearance of a man half his age. Younger. Had he not been plagued with gout he would, himself, have leapt to his feet and run to the window to see whether he could spot them with his own eyes. Instead, he deployed his daughter.

"No, Father." Amelia glanced obediently through the window and returned her attention to her book.

"How can you wait so patiently?" the admiral grumbled. "Are you not even the slightest bit excited about our promised trip?"

"I am!" Amelia laughed. "Of course I am. But I think you are excited enough for both of us."

Abandoning her attempt to read, she slipped Benjamin's leather bookmark in place and closed the book, allowing her fingers to rest a moment on the leather before sliding them free. He had been so kind to think of such a gift for her and she had been surprised that he had noticed her need of it. This realisation had, in turn, led her thoughts along a line they were not easily recalled from. That Sir Benjamin Devereaux noticed what she did, that he paid even the slightest attention to her activities ought not to have made colour seep into her cheeks, or caused her breath to catch, or -

"Milly, dear, are you alright?" Admiral Sudbury peered across the room at her, anxiety folding his features into themselves. "You look a little flushed. I hope you are not sickening for something..."

"No, indeed!" she said, hurriedly turning to smile at him. "I am quite well, Papa." Fearing that the promised treat day would be snatched away from her just as she had begun to look forward to it, she hurried to his side. "I was merely a little too caught up in my book."

"Pah!" the admiral waved away her explanation. "I wonder if I ought to object to your reading such novels if they are to have an effect on you. Too much emotion is not a good thing for a person, even if that person is a young lady." He affected a stern glance which he managed to maintain scarcely a moment before dissolving into laughter. "Fortunately you have inherited your father's logic along with your mama's sensitivity. Perhaps you are the best of us both." He patted her hand warmly and his voice grew weary. "I do not know what I shall do when you are married."

"Papa!"

"Do not cry *Papa* at me like that as if it is not a thought you yourself have had more than a few times. I myself encouraged it, although on days like today I cannot help but wonder why."

"*It is not good for man - or woman - to be alone,*" she quoted back to him in pious monotone, mocking the very words he had used to encourage her to pursue even the vaguest friendship with Mr Connelly.

"I said that did I?" the admiral grimaced. "And wherever did I glean that piece of wisdom?"

"It is from the Bible, Father!" Amelia laughed, merrily.

"Aye, well." Admiral Sudbury chuckled. "We all know how well acquainted I am with *that*." He paused, falling silent for a moment. The pressure of his hand on Amelia's softened, and when she looked at him she noticed he was scrutinising her closely. "I am glad you ignored my advice up 'til now," he remarked.

"Papa?" Amelia frowned at him.

"I thought marrying any fellow at all would be preferable to your not marrying anybody. I wonder if I was too hasty. Too -"

The sound of carriage wheels halted whatever else the admiral might have wished to say. As if a cloud had passed and allowed the sun to shine once more, he was his old self again.

"They're here!" He glanced at the clock on the mantel. "And precisely to time, as well! Come, come, my dear. Do not let us keep Sir Benjamin waiting." He hauled himself to his feet, and bustled from the room, tutting impatiently at the servant who had gone ahead of him to answer the door.

"Yes, yes!" He waved them away. "I know, Sir Benjamin's carriage is here. Devereaux!" he called, hurrying out into the bright morning sunlight, his cane in one hand and his hat in the other. "Good morning!"

"Good morning to you." Devereaux leapt out of the carriage and bowed in greeting to his neighbours. "Fine weather we have for our day's adventure, do not we?" He turned to Amelia, wearing a smile that was perhaps the most genuine she had seen on his handsome face. She could not resist returning it and was pleased to see it grow still wider in response.

"Yes, well. I am sure you did not drive all this way to stand on my doorstep!" Admiral Sudbury beamed at the two young people and offered his arm to Amelia. "Milly, dear."

Amelia allowed her father to help her into the carriage, feeling a strange glimmer of suspicion that to undertake that particular task had accounted for at least part of Sir Benjamin's determination to disembark at their entrance. His assistance was put to work in helping the admiral into the carriage, however, for Amelia's father was no longer the spry young man he had been in his youth. Presently, however, all were settled within the roomy Roland Park carriage, Amelia sitting comfortably beside her father and opposite Joanna. She noticed her friend was pressed quite uncomfortably into one corner of the seat, although Sir Benjamin took up no more than his half of the space. It was as if Joanna could not bear to risk any part of them coming into contact. Amelia frowned but Joanna met her eyes only briefly, before staring pointedly out of the window. It was Devereaux whose gaze found hers, his smile falling as he noticed her frown and misread it.

"Well, Miss Sudbury," he began, briskly rapping on the roof of the carriage with his knuckles. "I trust you will not find our day's visit too arduous."

"Arduous? How could we, when we travel in such luxury?" Admiral Sudbury remarked, leaning comfortably back in his seat. "Come, Amelia, and I will tell you a little of Malton, for I have an old friend who lodged there once upon a time...." He paused. "Bless me, I wonder if the fellow lives there still?"

"We shall endeavour to find out!" Devereaux said, evidently pleased to have this task upon which to hang their day. "It will give us gentlemen a goal for our day, whilst you ladies are perusing silk and lace." He rubbed his hands together in mimed glee. "Now, we must attend to another mater of extraordinarily important business. Where shall we stop along the way for our morning's refreshments?"

AMELIA WAS WITH THEM and for that Ben supposed he must be grateful. He could not help but wish she were at least half as pleased to be here as he was. He reclined in his seat, watching in silence as Mr Sudbury captured both young ladies' imaginations with an amazing tale of bravery from his youth in the navy. Amelia and Joanna's eyes were wide, and Ben congratulated himself for having the foresight to invite Amelia's father to accompany them, for it was impossible not to like the man, nor to marvel at his tales. He spoke with such a lack of artifice that Devereaux felt certain the tales were true and, if anything, Ben thought the admiral chose to play down his true heroics. Had the tale tripped from the lips of any of his London friends it would have been the other way, orchestrated to augment their bravery or heroism in the eyes of their impressionable feminine audience. Ben might have found such manipulation amusing - and often, he did laugh at the antics of his friends, however deplorable they might be in the cold light of day - he could not help but approve rather more of the admiral's honesty. Not for the first time, Ben regretted the use he had made of his liberty. His father might have cast him off unduly, but what benefit had he made of the condition?

Instead of pursuing sensible, rational acquaintances like the gentleman opposite, he had fallen in with a rash crowd. No, *fallen in* suggested he had done so quite by accident. He must confront his own ability to obscure the truth. He had sought out these particular friends and if the thought of less-than-noble antics reaching his father's ears registered with Ben at the time, it was with a sort of self-righteous indignation. His father already thought him capable of bad behaviour, well, then he would not disappoint! He had not fully anticipated the damage such rumours would do to his own reputation. Or had he realised, and simply chosen not to care? Those who had once been closest to him already believed the worst of him without caring to hear from his own lips that he was innocent. Let him merely confirm his father's worst suspicions, and enjoy himself in the meantime.

Idly, Ben's eyes slid across the carriage towards Amelia once more. It had not occurred to him that such rumours might prejudice another against him. He knew, however friendly he might imagine Amelia Sudbury to ever act towards him, she had already heard and believed the worst of him thanks to his sister. What hope had he of convincing her otherwise? Why bother to try?

Letting out a sigh, he turned towards the window, fixing his gaze on the trees that whipped past them. The audible sound must have reached Joanna's ears, for he felt his sister move on the bench seat next to him. He was wearying of whatever mood had possessed her these past few days and was in no humour to speak to her at present. His heart ached. They had been close, once upon a time. She had clung to his knees whenever he was home from school and referred to him as her dearest brother. She had cried when he was sent away. It had been her that his heart most hurt to leave behind and yet now she was his most avowed enemy, it seemed. Even her mother had softened, somehow, although he did not for a moment think that Lady Devereaux acted in anything but her own interests. He now possessed the familial purse-strings and she would, therefore, be as agreeable as possible in order to win his good favour. He snorted. She, too, was the one lady present in his life who knew the rumours about him to be false. She knew because she had created them. She had been responsible for feeding them to his father and ensuring that Benjamin Devereaux became the man he was today. If he must take responsibility for his own contribution to his current reputation, then so must his stepmother.

Their carriage reached the outskirts of town, and not a moment too soon. Ben did not like the melancholy turn his thoughts had taken. Not on a day that he had determined would be enjoyable.

"There is a pleasant inn hereabouts, what say we stop for a spot of refreshment first of all?" he asked, addressing his comment to the carriage at large, but resting his gaze on Admiral Sudbury. His friend - how much he felt as if he needed one with him just then! - beamed and agreed this would be a very good idea. Even Joanna seemed to acquiesce to this suggestion, for she smiled, leaning closer to Amelia and talking animatedly of the sorts of things they must look for in dresses if they were to be fully outfitted for the upcoming assembly. Ben could not help his eyes straying over to the two young ladies. He had been to more assemblies than they could contemplate and had become rather inured to their charm, particularly in

London, where the same crowds of people perpetually associated with one another.

He enjoyed them only insofar as he was able to spend time with this friends, and not one of them would be present at the upcoming country assembly. The thought ought to have soured Benjamin on the prospect but in truth, he could not help but feel a little excited at the thought. He would be free of the friends who influenced the worst parts of his nature, even if he could not be free of the rumours that alluded to it. He might have a chance, albeit a small one, of beginning again, beginning anew. He saw Amelia's eyes light up as she spoke in a low tone to her friend, and his own expression lifted into something approaching a smile. He had a reason, at least, to try.

Chapter Thirteen

The inn was crowded and between them, Devereaux and Admiral Sudbury succeeded in escorting their small party past at least one corner which housed a particularly boisterous card-game.

"Cheat!" one player hissed, jogging his companion on the shoulder. The accused made a vehement denial of the accusation and Ben found his attention drawn to their table. The man's back was to them, but he could not help but imagine it was Lennox sitting there, being accused of cheating at cards as he had been at so many tables in London. It had invariably been a call to Devereaux that he would need to intervene before Lennox was harmed physically for the damage his deceit had caused to his companion's purse. He scowled. Lennox was apparently incapable of playing a straight game of cards, without somehow endeavouring to rig the system, never mind any risk to his reputation or physical health.

Or to his friends! A muscle in Ben's jaw twitched, recalling more than one smarting blow he had received for coming to Lennox's aid. Not for the first time he wondered what his life would have been like had he not formed the friendships he had formed in London. How much safer. *And how much more dull!* One could not change the past, as well he knew. One had only the present and the promise of a future.

"Tell me, ladies, do you have firm ideas fixed in your minds of the purchases you wish to make?" he asked, reigniting the conversation and turning it, along with his own musings, to the safer topic of the approaching assembly and their immediate plans for the day ahead of them.

They had gathered around a small table and the serving staff were hurriedly bringing plates of food and pitchers of drinks enough to satisfy a small army, let alone a small group of four.

Amelia shook her head, opening her mouth to offer an answer but finding her quiet voice utterly drowned out at the sound of a cheer from the raucous card-table.

Ben frowned, wondering if they ought to have selected another table or another establishment altogether. There was no other option, now, for they were seated and with plates before them, yet he wondered if this error might sink him even further in his sister's, and thus her friend's, estimation. He had no more time to consider this, though, for Joanna raised her voice, quite willing and able to shout if it was required of her to be heard over the din.

"It is foolish to arrive with too fixed an opinion to a dressmaker," she observed, imperiously. "One never knows what one might come across."

"Indeed." The admiral nodded, sagely, although Ben could tell from the sparkle in his friend's eyes that he did not share Joanna's considered opinion. Clearly, neither gentleman was well-versed in the modes of fashion that most appealed to young ladies and for a trifling instant Ben almost missed his old friends.

Unbidden, his eyes strayed once more to the card table, and he grimaced. One fellow - he who had been accused of cheating and narrowly escaped a painful eviction from both game and inn - had his back turned towards them, his face obscured by shadow. There was something strangely familiar about the fellow's posture, though, the way he tilted his head one way and then another, surveying his opponents. Devereaux's mind conjured up the expression the man would be wearing if it were indeed George Lennox and the picture was so accurate and intoxicating that for a moment Ben felt as if he had conjured a spectre. It took him a moment longer when the fellow chanced to turn, to acknowledge that this was not imagination but reality. The gambler was not merely an image of George Lennox – he was Lennox in the flesh. In shock, Ben turned back to his meal, angling his chair a little so that his shoulders turned away from the table, minimising the chance that his friend would see him in turn. *What is he doing here?* he wondered, furiously. *He will not wish to see me, surely?*

Joanna continued to debate aloud the virtues of Belgian lace over French, but Devereaux scarcely heard a word. His ears were tuned acutely to the card table, to the voice he now isolated and identified as belonging to George Lennox. He recognised the patter he had heard practised in and out of almost every gaming hall in London.

"Is something the matter, Sir Benjamin?"

It was Amelia's voice that broke through his confusion, pulling him back to the table before him instead of one several feet away. He looked at her and saw real concern etched into her delicate features.

"Not a thing, Miss Sudbury!" he responded, cheerfully. It was artifice and somehow she seemed to know it, for the light dimmed in her pale eyes and she nodded, very slightly, before turning back to Joanna and offering the name of a particular shade of green her friend struggled to pinpoint.

Ben's heart sank. He had lied, and Amelia knew he had, yet what was the alternative? To confess that he recognised the man branded "cheat" but a few moments before? Not only that but to confess he, himself, had been party to such deceit on more evenings than he could remember? There would be no way to prevent Lennox inviting himself to join them, in that instance, and if there was one thing Ben remained determined to insist upon it was keeping these two parts of his life entirely separate. What hope had he of convincing Amelia Sudbury that he was not the rake she thought him if she met his friend?

He returned to his dinner, taking a morose mouthful of a stew that had suddenly become tasteless and gristly, souring along with his mood. He swallowed, putting the thought of his friend out of his mind. Perhaps it was not Lennox at all. No, indeed, now that he considered it he thought it likely that he had only looked *like* George Lennox, and Ben, struck by the similarity to the friend he knew well and merely filled in the blanks and conjured up the spectre of his friend in the very position he knew he would have been likely to occupy. Malton was a tiny town, and Lennox knew nobody who lived there. Why on earth would he forsake London for such a place?

Pursuing this logical line of thought, his spirits rose and he found his appetite returning as he attended with more vigour to his meal. He even managed to offer a word or two in contribution to the young ladies' discussion - blue, indeed, was always a pretty colour, and he had never yet met a gentleman who disliked it. He began to look forward to the promise of the afternoon ahead of them when, all of a sudden, a heavy hand clamped down on his shoulder and he heard a familiar, tuneless laugh ring mere inches from his ears.

"Devereaux! I thought that was you. I was on my way to pay you a visit at your estate but I see Providence has contrived to intercede and meet us first. What a charming table you have! Don't suppose there's room for another?"

⚜

JOANNA HAD EVIDENTLY been less than delighted by the arrival of Devereaux's friend, for not long after Mr George Lennox was invited to join their table, she turned quite pointedly to Amelia and announced that they ought to make haste to the haberdashers, lest their entire journey be wasted. Amelia, uncertain of leaving the gentlemen, had lingered. Devereaux himself seemed rather less than enamoured by his friend's arrival, although he did not refuse the fellow a chair and strove to make introductions as warmly as possible. He did not seem himself, though, and she wondered if it was the presence of his friend or the fact that he had been found by his friend in their company that was responsible for his apparent discomfort. Apparent was all it must have been, Amelia thought, for neither Joanna nor her father, nor even Mr Lennox, seemed to think there was anything at all the matter with Benjamin Devereaux. Only she, Amelia, noticed the way his eyes clouded, the muscle in his jaw that twitched as if he were clenching his teeth tightly closed, the back which was slightly too straight to enable him to appear quite as relaxed as he wished.

Admiral Sudbury seemed to notice her hesitancy, however, and misread it.

"Amelia! Allow me to accompany you both, for I am sure Sir Benjamin is eager to reconnect with his old friend. Jolly good to make your acquaintance, Mr Lennox. Devereaux." He beamed at the two fellows, waving his cane at them, and offered an arm to each lady. Amelia laughed and slipped her hand into the crock of his elbow but Joanna refused, with a polite smile, and came around to Amelia's other side.

"As you wish, Miss Devereaux," the admiral said, cheerfully, as the party of three made their way out into the bustling street. "I dare say this way is all for the best, for I need my cane a good deal more than I care to acknowledge." He grimaced and limped but before Amelia could enquire after his health she deduced he was exaggerating the motion for the sake of humour and jabbed him good-naturedly in his substantial side.

"Have you met Mr Lennox before, Joanna?" Amelia asked, as they put a little distance between them and the inn behind them. She was intrigued, now, to know the nature of the friendship between Mr Lennox and Sir Benjamin, for they certainly seemed to be close, despite Devereaux's conflicted feelings at their reunion.

Joanna shook her head, fiercely.

"He is one of the four horsemen, I suppose." She arched both eyebrows, engaging Amelia in silent conversation. *Do you see now why I despaired so of his coming to Westham? Just think of the trouble he will cause, bringing all his friends amongst us. This is merely the beginning...*

"Four Horsemen?" Admiral Sudbury looked to both ladies for an explanation. "What four horsemen? Mr Lennox did not strike me as an equestrian..."

"No, Papa!" Amelia swallowed a laugh and patted his arm. "It is merely a nickname. One that Sir Benjamin - ah one that has been applied to several in Sir Benjamin's circle. His London friends."

"Four of them, presumably," the admiral grumbled. "Well, two others, if we count Devereaux as one and this Lennox fellow as another." He raised his own eyebrows, but the expression was one of amusement rather than the horror of Joanna's. "I can just imagine what horrors they got up to that won them such a name." He chuckled. "Tell me, which one is poor Devereaux? Famine, perhaps? Death?" He shuddered to humorous effect and was lost in his own amusement for several steps before he realised that neither young lady found the matter quite so funny.

"Yes, well. I dare say it is nowhere near as bad as the gossip-mongers would have us believe. One ought to judge a man on his behaviour, not on what is said about him."

"And what if one has not seen enough of him to judge his behaviour?" It was Joanna who voiced this question, the very one that had been on the tip of Amelia's tongue to ask. She ducked her head, waiting for her father's response in hopes that his wisdom would offer her some way out of the conflicted feelings she currently bore towards Joanna's brother. Whether to despise him, judge him, avoid him, the same way his sister seemed determined to do or to yield to her heart which stubbornly refused to accept he was quite the devil her friend believed him to be. Fate seemed determined to offer confusing evidence on either side, and Amelia could make neither head nor tail of it, nor of Devereaux himself.

"One might consider reserving one's judgment until one *has* witnessed enough of his behaviour in person so as to make a true determination." Admiral Sudbury's voice had softened. "My dear Joanna, a great deal has happened to your brother that you are perhaps not privy to, for good and ill. I do not necessarily advocate a young lady knowing all of a gentleman's history." He cleared his throat. "Too much brandy can lead even the most sensible fellow into a scrape - not that I speak from personal experience, you understand." He winked, hard, and Amelia felt his hold tighten encouragingly on her. "But a few mistakes in a gentleman's past ought not to rob him of his future. It is unpopular to voice such an opinion, I suppose, but you forget, Miss Devereaux, that my past is different from yours. I have earned my wealth and my position through my own hard-won victories both at home and abroad." His voice grew taut. "There are a great many members of society who would dismiss me the same way they would your brother and consider us unworthy of association simply because of our pasts."

"Untrue!" Joanna argued. "Why, Admiral Sudbury, anybody alive can see that you are worthy of respect -"

"My dear Miss Devereaux, you have not been to London nor had cause to associate with a good deal of our wider society. I assure you that not everybody shares your good opinion of the navy. I dare say, were we in London at the moment you would find many more doors open to Sir Benjamin and his fellow horsemen than would ever be open to me or my family. I do not say this to earn your sympathy, merely as a point of consideration." He paused as they drew within sight of a street of shops. "But look, here we are at the haberdashery already, and I am scarcely begun on my lecture. Forgive me, ladies, I will hold the rest of it in readiness. For now, you have more pressing concerns than the mere function of society." He lowered his voice, with a conspiratorial grin. "Let us turn our attention instead to the highly contentious topic of...hair-ribbons!"

Chapter Fourteen

"I was thinking it would do me some good to get out of London for a little while too. And visiting you seemed to be the perfect opportunity!"

Lennox was talking quickly and loudly, although Devereaux did not think he was aware of the edge in his voice or manner.

"How much do you owe?" he asked, in a low voice. Lennox might hold to the explanation of a desire for fresh country air all he chose, but Ben knew him too well to believe it.

"A little," Lennox allowed, taking another sip of his drink, and eyeing the half-empty plates with undisguised hunger. With a sigh, Ben waved a servant over and ordered a fresh plate for his friend, certain that, if Lennox's debts were as bad as he anticipated, it might have been days since he had eaten anything substantial.

"Where are the others?" he asked, wondering why their two companions had not come to Lennox's aid. Merriweather and Stephens had their faults, but losses at the card tables were not usually amongst them.

Lennox looked crestfallen.

"Merriweather is lost to me. He only has eyes for Miss Bertram and you know how hopeless he is when he is in love. He fears being seen associating with me will only harm his chances of securing the young lady's affections." He grimaced. "Or, more accurately, those of her guardian. Stephens refuses to help me simply because he claims he has helped me too often already, to no avail." He cracked a smile. "He told me I will not change until I am forced to, and he is forcing me to."

Ben raised his eyebrows, waiting a moment before responding. His silence did as he hoped and Lennox hurried out an explanation of his behaviour that day.

"I know, I am not showing much evidence of changing, forced or not. I ought not to have run straight for the nearest card table but you don't understand, Dev. I'm down to my last farthing. How else was I supposed to go on? I could not turn up at your door with nothing. What if you refused to see me?"

Ben let out a low sigh.

"If you thought such a reception likely, you were foolish to attempt the journey." His friend looked so weary and beaten down that he could not find it in himself to be stern. He reached out a hand and clapped it lightly on his shoulder. "Of course you are welcome to stay with me. But you ought to have written. I could have sent some money, or..." He shrugged. "Something. I could have helped." He grimaced. "Now that I am in a position to." He swallowed the natural objections that rose in his throat at such an assertion. He was wealthier than he had been, certainly, but that did not mean his own purse was a bottomless pit to be raided by all of his friends and family members. Was that not precisely the problem he had in dealing with his stepmother? Lady Devereaux seemed utterly oblivious to the fact that her husband had been a spendthrift and a poor manager, leaving the estate depleted and in need of investment he did not have. Devereaux had a title, yes, but if he hoped to keep it he would need to retrench, not take on even greater financial responsibility. He scowled, knowing precisely what his friends would advocate in such a position. To a man, they would remind Ben of his skills. Handsome and charming, when he chose to be, he was exceptionally capable of securing a way out of financial straits easily, if only he chose to do it. He could marry some wealthy young woman with a dowry well able to secure the future of Roland Park. The idea would have seemed practical to him before, albeit a little unsavoury. He would justify it to himself with the assertion that love was a habit, not an emotion, at least not outside of novels which played up romance into a fallacy of a thing. He would choose to love whatever wife he married and if he could be clear-headed enough to see that he could be clear-headed enough to make a sensible choice.

However. He frowned. Since then he had met Amelia Sudbury. He had claimed, since his return to Roland Park that he was a changed man. Could it be that the very act of returning to Roland Park was what had changed him? No longer did he care to prove his father wrong, or to revel in the reputation that had been foisted upon him and prove his absent father right. No longer did he think love a mere habit. How could he marry another woman when Amelia Sudbury was in existence? Yet alas, how could he marry Amelia Sudbury who had nought but whatever small dowry her admiral father might bestow upon her? It would be better than nothing, certainly, but hardly enough to secure his languishing estate.

"What are you thinking of?" Lennox asked, his words obscured by a mouthful of meat. He chewed and swallowed with relish, before pausing long enough to prompt his friend into replying. "Rethinking your generosity?" He elbowed Ben in the side and winked. "Worried I'll ruin your spotless reputation?"

Ben snorted. Lennox knew, perhaps more than most, the tattered state of Benjamin Devereaux's reputation in and around Westham. He had contributed to its ruination by dragging Ben into his exploits in London. Yet, despite possessing a tarnished reputation all his own, being talked of in hushed, horrified whispers by dowagers and wallflowers alike never seemed to bother George Lennox. Ben grimaced. Perhaps because his reputation, however poor, had been deserved. He had earned every whisper, every withering stare, every rumour that swirled around him. Devereaux's misdeeds were a fabrication and yet he was held to account for them, despite never having had the enjoyment of committing the acts that now hung about him like medals, earning him scorn instead of praise.

"I am more worried my reputation will ruin you!" he remarked, downing the last of his drink and setting his mug down. "You have heard me talk of my dear stepmother. Well this afternoon, Lennox, you shall meet her." He grinned. "I dread to think what you will make of one another. Perhaps that alone will be worth the price of paying your debts. Give me a list, and I shall do all I can to settle it." He held up his hand. "No, do not attempt to talk me out of it or make hollow promises that you will pay me back. We need not speak of it any more. You shall change, or you shall not, but on this occasion, I shall not allow your past mistakes to burden your future." He grew serious. "*You* ought not to allow your past mistakes to burden your future. You have a life in front of you, Lennox. Why not begin fresh, now, and see where it takes you?"

⚜

"THERE IS SCARCELY A circumstance or feeling that cannot be improved by the purchase of a new dress!" Joanna declared, clutching her chit close to her chest as if it were the dress itself.

Amelia smiled, faintly, although she could not hope to match her friend's enthusiasm. She had made her own selection, more at the insistence of her friend and her father than of any interest within her. She never considered herself a young lady that lived for fashion, which was a very good thing, living as she did in a household of at least one clueless older gentleman, but even she was not immune to the thrill of new silk, lace and ribbons. That day, however, the thrill fell flat.

"What is the matter?" Joanna whispered, evidently noticing her miserable expression. "You do not regret your choice, surely? That pale blue is most becoming on you, Milly! Think about how it will sparkle in the candlelight at the assembly. You will be ethereal, and certain to catch the eye of every eligible gentleman present!" She paused as if reflecting a little unhappily on the truth of this declaration. She tossed her head. "You shall not outshine me, of course, but together we will surely charm the whole room!"

She paused, glancing surreptitiously in Amelia's direction and speaking again as if the idea had just occurred to her.

"You are certain to catch the eye of any gentleman you might wish. Whoever has won your heart...for I wager there is just such a one, whoever he might be."

Amelia said nothing, waiting for the topic to draw to a close, but Joanna had the bit between her teeth and took silence as encouragement.

"I hope there is someone you like, even if you wish to keep his existence a secret. It suggests you will not be taken in by my dreadful brother!"

Amelia's heart quickened and she lifted her eyes to Joanna's to see if her friend had noticed. She was too intent on her words, though, warming to her subject with every moment she devoted to it. Amelia could never be so foolish as to develop an affection for the *dreadful Sir Benjamin*, yet with every reason Joanna offered against such a possibility, Amelia was increasingly forced to acknowledge its truth. She *did* care for Sir Benjamin Devereaux. He was clever and amusing and had experienced so much of life that Amelia had only ever dreamed of or read about. Yes, even Joanna's dire warnings of scandal and bad behaviour were no longer enough to deter Amelia's heart from knowing better. She let out a sigh that did not fail to reach her friend's hearing.

"I would understand a stranger falling in love with him, I suppose," Joanna acknowledged as if conceding Amelia a point she had not made. "He is quite - quite handsome, after all, and I dare say he can be very charming when he wishes to be." She paused. "But that is not the sort of love one ought to encourage. I only tell you this because I care for you, dear, you understand that. I do not wish for you to have your heart broken." Her eyes flashed. "And I certainly do not wish to see you married to such a dreadful man. Imagine a lifetime of living with his terrible behaviour. It would be enough to drive a woman to madness!" She shook her head. "I wish for someone altogether better for you, my dear."

"Like Mr Connelly?" Amelia remarked, sourly. She had never quite been agreeable to the notion of forming anything beyond friendship with the curate, in spite of her father's encouragement, but now the very idea of allying herself with him when she knew Sir Benjamin Devereaux existed in the world was painful. *I would rather be a spinster all my days!*

Joanna, however, did not see the problem, nor did she seem to notice Amelia's disappointment at the notion of a future on Mr Connelly's arm. She brightened, clutching her friend closer as they continued their leisurely walk.

"Yes! Oh, wouldn't you make a perfect curate's wife? You would be so comfortable and welcoming, and nobody could fail but to come from your home without feeling suitably cheered."

"That is all I can hope for, you think?" Amelia knew her friend meant well, but it was not the first time Joanna had offered an insult disguised as a compliment. She did not want a life of parish visits and homemaking and *comfort*. She wished for a little adventure – the same kind of adventure she had found in the pages of her book. Her father had had some – yes, and Mama too, for she had travelled right along with her husband before Arthur was born. Arthur had travelled to places Amelia could scarcely pronounce and his adventuring spirit was encouraged, if not lauded! Why must she be forced to contain hers, to keep her imagination limited to other people's stories, created by other people's pens?

Her silence, again, was enough to encourage Joanna to continue.

"Why, it is a great deal to hope for, do not you think? A home of your own, and a husband who adores you." The thought of Mr Connelly ever expressing any emotion close to adoration for anything beyond the sound of his own voice must have struck Joanna as absurd, as it did Amelia, and she modified her words. "That is, he will love you as much as it is proper for a gentleman to love his wife." Pulling her friend closer, she smiled. "I dare say there is no man alive good enough to win the affections of my dear friend Amelia, yet in winning your heart he will raise several places in my own estimation. Yes. I think he will take one look at you in your new dress and propose on the spot. You see if he does not!"

This little speech was designed to cheer her friend and Amelia wished she *could* be so easily cheered out of her strange temper, but she could not help but feel weighed down by Joanna's words, the imagined future she laid out before her like a mat. Amelia's eyes swam with tears and she hurried to blink them back. It was foolishness, for she could not imagine worldly Sir Benjamin could ever care for her. Nothing had changed. Her future remained precisely as it had before he came to Westham. Yet, for Amelia, everything was different. She reached a hand up to wipe away her tears, hoping Joanna would not notice, but her friend had the eyes of an eagle and she forced Amelia to look at her.

"My dear Amelia! Do you not *want* to be married?"

Joanna spoke as if there could be nothing worse in all creation, and the reminder of their difference on this particular point was just what was needed to recall Amelia to herself. She smiled, her remaining tears giving way to the very lightest of laughs.

"You know I have never been so very set on it as you have, Josie, dear." She shook her head, her curls bobbing with the motion. "But it is not marriage in the abstract that causes me such dismay. It is..." She paused, drawing in one more fortifying breath before choking out the words she knew she must say aloud, though they might bring her the ridicule of her friend, perhaps even her disdain.

"I do not wish to marry Mr Connelly," Amelia confessed. "I do not think I ever have wished to marry him. But now - now I know I never can."

"Why?" Joanna was mystified. "Is he so very bad? Or -" Here, her eyes narrowed. "Is there someone else who you prefer? Some other gentleman who has stolen your heart." Her voice took on a strange, flattened note as if she already knew what Amelia would say before she spoke a word. Still, Amelia spoke. She knew she must, and she knew she could trust her friend to keep her secret. Joanna had made no secret of the war of silence and attrition that still raged between herself and her brother: she would not betray Amelia's confidence to him, so he might never come to know of her folly. There was some comfort in that. Wetting her lips, Amelia spoke, her words little more than a whisper.

"I am afraid so, Joanna," Amelia confessed, her lips white. "It is foolishness, for I know he can never care for me, nor should I wish him to, but - but I fear I shall never love another."

"Who is this villain?" Joanna asked, affecting a light-heartedness she evidently did not feel. "For if he does not love you I shall plague him mercilessly until he does. Surely he cannot know you at all if he is not smitten with you already, but if he needs persuasion you may rest assured, Milly, I shall endeavour to do it."

Amelia's voice dropped still lower and her response came only after a surreptitious glance over her shoulder had reassured her she would not be overheard by the admiral, who had paused to admire some pretty little folly and was now increasing his pace in order that he might close the distance between himself and the young ladies, as their party continued their journey back to the inn.

"It is your brother."

Chapter Fifteen

If the journey out to Malton had been a strained one then the journey back verged on painful. Amelia, seated next to her father, kept her pale gaze fixed on the passing scenery. Her features seemed strangely drawn for reasons Benjamin could not begin to fathom. If Admiral Sudbury noticed his daughter's apparent change in mood, he did not remark upon it, instead, he occupied himself in getting to know George Lennox better. Ben must give his friend due respect for managing himself admirably. He seemed to have sensed without needing to be told that these new acquaintances of Devereaux's were not the same as he might have formed in London and must be treated with due deference and respect, and not shocked unduly by recounting tales of daring and scandal. Even more to Ben's relief, Lennox seemed to have become an entirely new person himself, showing only the kindest, most agreeable parts of his nature and enquiring warmly for more intelligence of Westham, a small place about which he had no knowledge.

The other gentlemen of the party thus occupied, Ben felt free to turn his attention to the ladies. Amelia, it seemed to him, was pointedly avoiding being drawn into conversation, in fact, she seemed most pointedly to be avoiding *him*. Now, even, she turned away, angling her whole body as well as her gaze apart from him. Joanna, by contrast, stared in his direction as if she could subdue him merely by looking. It was a change from being ignored, but not necessarily a welcome one.

"Well, ladies," he began. He met Joanna's gaze, determined not to be cowed into silence in his own carriage. "Was your visit to Malton a successful one? I do not see any bundles or bags. Do not tell me the haberdashery remains unscathed?" He smiled, turning his eyes to Amelia but she did not look at him and his expression dropped.

"They will send on after us." Joanna's voice was taut as if she spoke through gritted teeth. "Once they have completed any necessary making up."

"Of course." Ben nodded, sliding his eyes back to her. She had not moved, had not lessened the scowl she kept fixed on him. He got the distinct impression that she was angry with him but could not fathom why now should be any different to her previous indifference. She had transformed from silence and ignorance to simmering rage. Surely there must be a reason for such a change but he could not understand it. *Nor do I care to!* Yet, even as he had this thought, his gaze travelled once more to Amelia and his heart sank. If he could be certain that Joanna's change in opinion had nothing to do with her, he would dismiss it as merely the whim of his highly strung sister and leave her to her rage, expecting the mood to blow itself out in time. But Amelia seemed to have caught whatever wind of discontent had blown through Joanna and the usually conversational Miss Sudbury had become a shadow of her former self. Ben's eyes narrowed. Had she been crying? He had been at the mercy of ladies' tears often enough that he had thought himself immune to them. That was in London, though, when tears were but one weapon in an arsenal ladies might deploy against him. On Miss Sudbury, their appearance was far more devastating, and it was all Ben could do to restrain himself from reaching across the carriage to take Amelia's hand and bid her tell him what was the matter.

Miss Sudbury, he corrected himself, silently. *Not Amelia.* He must stop this foolishness of thinking of her as anything more than his friend's daughter. If she considered any member of the Devereaux household a friend in her own right it was not him, but his sister and a lady less inclined to recommend him to Amelia scarcely existed in all of England.

A frown settled over his brow, her discomfort a mystery impossible to solve. He turned his attention as best he could to the gentlemen, who had moved from Lennox's cleverly edited personal history to Admiral Sudbury's. Ben always enjoyed hearing his friend speak of his travels and although he had heard many of these stories before, this did not stop his attention being caught once more by tales of bravery, both on the battlefront and at the mercy of trade winds. He thought himself well-travelled, but compared to the admiral he was provincial indeed and even Lennox seemed to appreciate his tales.

"What a life you have lived, sir!" George said, laughing over an explanation of the difficulties of communicating with a people without the aid of a common language. "It makes life in London seem dull indeed!"

"If you think London dull, George, I feel I must warn you about the pace of life in the country," Ben said, with an easy smile. "I fear you will hardly know what to do with yourself, or how to occupy your time. There is nought to do but walk, or ride, or read." Ben let out a long, luxurious sigh as if to acknowledge that such an existence was, to him, a small slice of paradise. Lennox looked at him sideways, a mischievous grin dancing about his thin lips.

"I would never have imagined such a life satisfying for one such as you, Devereaux." He arched an eyebrow. "But now that I see a small sampling of the company one might expect to keep whilst indulging in such simple pleasures, I can see how wrong I have been."

Ben frowned, willing colour not to flood his cheeks and so to betray him. Lennox had scarcely met Amelia, yet already, somehow, he seemed to have seen through Devereaux's studied disinterest to deduce, truthfully, that if there was one part of life in Westham that Ben valued above all others, it was the acquaintance of a particular young lady. One who at present could hardly bear to turn her eyes towards him for even a moment.

"You tease us, Mr Lennox," Joanna said, frostily. "I am quite sure such simple young ladies as we can scarcely begin to compete with your London circles." The comment was innocent but delivered with just enough scorn that both Devereaux and Lennox understood her disapproval. It was a page from the Lady Devereaux manual of behaviour, and Ben barely managed to keep from rolling his eyes. Would he never strip Joanna back from the cruel, cantankerous young lady she had become to the merry sister he remembered from ten years ago? Had she really changed so much in his absence?

"Father!" Amelia's voice came, so sudden and so unexpected that all eyes turned towards her. She lifted a shaking hand toward the window. "Were you expecting callers today? Look, there is a carriage I do not recognise. Its occupants - why - why Papa!" Her shock turned to delight, and she turned a shining smile on Ben, his companion and at last, her father. "Arthur is here! He has come to see us!"

AMELIA BARELY WAITED for the carriage to slow before she was hurrying to open the carriage door. Devereaux was quicker, reaching for the handle and opening the door before she could manage to wrap her fingers around it He stepped out first, too, holding his hand up to help her out She took it almost without realising, for at that moment her attention was entirely occupied with another gentleman. As her feet touched the ground she flew to him, seeing in the tall, broad-shouldered man in the garden her own brother, home again after so many years.

"Arthur!" she cried, hurling herself into his arms.

"Well hello, Amelia!" He laughed, swinging her around in a circle. "Why are you so surprised to see me? Did you not get my letter?"

Admiral Sudbury had hurried quite quickly after his daughter and greeted his son with a no less enthusiastic shake of the hand.

"What letter, eh? You are teasing your old Pa!" He beamed at his son, continuing to pump his arm up and down far longer than was necessary.

"Ah, I come in advance of it." Arthur looked as if he wished to embrace both sister and father at once, but a movement at the periphery of his vision halted the impulse, and he took a step back, straightening almost imperceptibly as he acknowledged the carriage that still held the rest of their party, save for Devereaux, who hung back, eyeing the reunion with a peculiar expression on his face.

"Who is this fierce fellow, Milly? He looks rather as if he might like to murder me."

"Arthur!" Amelia socked him on the arm and turned towards Devereaux, her momentary delight at having her brother back displacing all the riot of emotion that had been at war within her for the duration of their journey. Looking at their neighbour caused her happiness to falter but not fail completely, for he, reading the situation in an instant, took a step forward to be introduced.

"Our neighbour, Arthur," Admiral Sudbury said, drawing Devereaux closer. "He is but lately returned to Westham too. My, what a time for reunions we are having! Devereaux, this is my son, Captain Arthur Sudbury."

"Pleased to meet you," Arthur said, with a self-satisfied beam. He shook Devereaux's hand heartily, and Amelie's attention had been so fixed on this first meeting between the two gentlemen that it took her a moment to look back at her brother.

"How long will you stay?" she asked. "We did not expect you for some time yet."

"Aye." Arthur laughed. "It was thought that I'd earned myself some leave and so here I am, ready to enjoy my spoils."

A momentary shadow flickered across his features but before Amelia could question it, Devereaux spoke again.

"Well, I shall not stand in the way of a family reunion." He bowed once more, resting his eyes on Amelia as he straightened. "I shall bid you farewell, Miss Sudbury. Captain

Sudbury. Admiral." He waved and returned to his carriage. Amelia watched the vehicle lurch into motion before she could tear her eyes from it, and return them to her brother.

"I cannot believe you are truly here!" she exclaimed, tucking her arm through his and leading him into the house. Admiral Sudbury preceded them, bustling servants out of the way and making for the parlour, demanding they be brought tea and a *hearty repast* for the returning sea-farer. "Are you really here to say?"

"As long as you'll have me!" Arthur said, cheerily. "I am tired of living a bachelor life and enduring life aboard ship. I am ready to embrace some home comforts." He arched an eyebrow, dropping his voice so that he could be certain his words were not overheard by their father. "I had not realised I would be in danger of upsetting your own pursuit of the comforts of another home. Devereaux...he is heir to Roland Park, is not he?"

"He is its owner." Amelia blushed, wishing her brother had not fixed so shrewd a glance upon her. "The old Sir Benjamin died, Arthur. This is the new."

"Indeed. Well, he is a good deal more handsome than his father, I suppose." Arthur wrinkled his nose as if considering the matter carefully.

"Arthur!" Amelia poked him.

"Oh, do not tell me you haven't noticed. I dare say he has noticed *you*, or did I imagine the careful way he handed you out of the carriage? The poor fellow looked quite upset when you shoved him aside and ran to greet me. 'Tis a good job you introduced me quickly enough as your brother or I've a notion he might have challenged me to a duel."

"If you mean to tease me before you have been here even half an hour I shall begin to wish you had stayed at sea!" Amelia said, primly.

"Very well!" Arthur held up his hands in mock surrender. "I shall reserve my teasing for when I am fully settled. But do not imagine this matter dismissed, sister dear. I know Father tries but he is far less suspicious than he ought to be. I am only too aware of gentlemen's intentions when they come across a fair maiden such as yourself." He scowled and puffed out his chest as if spoiling for a fight. "I am not yet sure how I feel about Sir Benjamin, however new and handsome he may be, making a claim on my sister."

"He has done no such thing," Amelia protested, though her voice shook a little as she did so, and she prayed Arthur would not notice. "He is a friend, scarcely even that! I am better acquainted with his sister, although he has become quite an avid visitor to Papa."

"Indeed?" Arthur's low voice suggested he did not think *Papa* was the only, or even most important, reason Devereaux might have taken to calling at their home at regular intervals, but he did not say as much out loud.

"He is more used to London society," Amelia equivocated. "What on earth could he possibly see in me?"

She let out a breath she was not aware of having held, but in uttering the words aloud it was as if she reminded herself of their truth. She might have foolishly lost her heart over handsome, devilish Devereaux, but there was no chance of her affections being returned. The sooner she accepted the truth of that particular matter, the better.

"Anyway, I do not wish to talk about life in Westham, there is time enough for that. Tell me about you!" She beamed, seating her brother. "Tell me all about your journey. When did you return to England? Where is your ship? What are your plans now?"

Chapter Sixteen

The rain had begun scarcely after the party had back arrived at Roland Park, and Ben was glad that they had not delayed their return journey too long. It would have been dreadful to travel in such weather as this. Lost in his thoughts, the sound of raindrops hammering on the glass behind him slowly faded from his notice.

"Arthur!"

Ben had been replaying the image of Amelia hurling herself into her brother's arms almost without ceasing, since their return to Roland Park. He had introduced Lennox to his stepmother and then retired to his study on the pretence of attending to some estate business. In reality, the ledger lay open before him but he did not see a single line of it. All he saw, over and over again, was the difference in Amelia Sudbury between when she looked at him and when she looked at her brother. His stomach roiled with jealousy, but was he jealous that she could ever look at another man so warmly - in which, case it was foolishness, for the fellow was her brother and thus entitled to a degree of affection - or was it was because he, brother to a sister himself, had never received such a welcome.

Joanna seemed to be likewise unnerved by the picture of delight they had witnessed. Oh, she had not said as much but he wagered, as they travelled the short distance between

Amelia's home and Roland Park, that her gaze had become less scathing and sadder as she fixed it upon him.

There was a light tap at his door, and he barked out a terse response.

"Yes?"

To his surprise when the door opened it was not to admit Lennox, as he had expected, but Joanna herself. Ben blinked, curious to be faced with the young woman who had so recently been at the forefront of his memory.

"Mama asked me to check with you whether the blue room would be acceptable lodgings for your friend. Shall I tell the servants to take him up?"

"Yes, that will be quite adequate," he muttered, dropping his eyes back to his ledger. Joanna did not leave immediately, though, and he looked up at her again. "Is anything else the matter?"

Joanna darted a glance over her shoulder, apparently debating something. At last, she shook herself, almost imperceptibly, and took a light step over the threshold and into Ben's study. Her entrance into his own private domain was so unexpected - welcome, but unexpected - that Benjamin straightened in his chair, fixing a cautious glance on her.

"Joanna?" he prompted. "Is something the matter?"

"It was raining," Joanna said, quietly. She would not look at him but kept her eyes fixed on some point on the ground. Her words tumbled out one after another as if she was scarcely aware of thinking them before she spoke them aloud. "It felt as if it had been raining forever and it was so cold and dark. I did not want you to go out in that without a coat, or -" She paused, biting her lip. "I did not want you to go out in that. I couldn't understand why everyone was so angry. Nobody would tell me. Mama told me to go up to bed, but she sent me with Abigail and not Mary so I knew something was the matter. She had disappeared, and nobody would tell me where she had gone, and I heard shouting so I crept downstairs to see what was the matter."

She lifted her eyes, then, and fixed them on him.

"Why didn't you just apologise? Why not try to make it up? It was a mistake. Papa would have been angry, but he would have forgiven you."

Ben smiled, sadly.

"I fear you did not know our father well if you think that, Jo." He had used her pet-name by accident, but for once she didn't stiffen and shy away at the familiarity of the sound. Instead, she crept closer, folding herself carefully into the chair opposite him.

"Do you love her?" she asked, quietly. "Did you ever?"

"Who?" Ben's mind raced into overdrive. At first, he had thought the lady Joanna spoke of was Amelia, and he wondered how it was that his sister, too, had so easily deduced his feelings. He had practised so often and for so long to keep them well hidden and yet here, in Westham, his true feelings seemed to be apparent to all except the one lady he most wished to share them with. Joanna continued, dragging his mind from the present back ten years to the night she had first begun describing.

"Mary Bell."

Ben's grip tightened on his pen, and he laid it down, fearing, then, that he might snap it, so visceral was his reaction to hearing the name of the young woman who had destroyed his relationship with his father. He grimaced. No, it had not been Miss Bell's fault. She had been merely a pawn. It was his stepmother who had manoeuvred her into place, who had constructed the lie that his sister, now, was demanding the truth of.

"I hardly knew her," he said, honestly. "I certainly did not love her, either then or now."

"Then why throw everything away for her?" Joanna's voice grew soft, sad. "Why leave us?"

"Recall, sister, it was not my desire to leave," he muttered, grimly, recalling the anger that had flashed in his father's eyes when he demanded an accounting from Ben that the young man could not give. He had heard stories, he claimed, tales told by the servants. He would not endure such gossip or such behaviour in his own house. Even now, Ben was not sure whether his father had been more enraged by the notion that his son had seduced Joanna's governess or the idea that it was being discussed by other people. He certainly did not care to hear that the story was an utter fabrication and dismissed any attempt Ben made to tell him as much.

Will you call your mother a liar? he had raged, storming around this very room.

She is not my mother. These words had been the last straw for Sir Benjamin Devereaux senior, and Ben had known it. His father had grown very still and very quiet all of a sudden and when next he spoke it was as if he was conducting simply a matter of business, not evicting his own son from the only home he had ever known.

Then perhaps this is not your home, either. You can go to London, Benjamin. I have business you might attend to there and I am sure you will be eager to make your own way in the world of London society rather than in the bosom of the family you evidently despise.

He drew a breath, surprised that it shook, and lifted his gaze to Joanna's.

"I do not suppose you will believe it, but would you care to hear the truth of what happened that night, Josie? I will tell you, to the best of my memory, why I left, but I wager you will not like it." He smiled, grimly, and began.

<hr>

"AND YOU ARE HAPPY FOR it, father?"

Amelia heard Arthur's voice as she tiptoed downstairs in search of the book she had forgotten upon first retiring to her room. It was late and she had gone to bed, leaving her father and brother to sit up in Admiral Sudbury's study, drinking brandy (her father) and smoking (Arthur) and talking. She ought not to eavesdrop and indeed she scarcely intended to, but for the reply that came in her father's weary tone.

"Amelia may love whomever she wishes."

"But that fellow?" Arthur snorted. "I assume you have heard the stories -"

"I am surprised you have!" the admiral replied. "Did you linger in London simply to gather information on our newest neighbour, when you might have come here directly and discovered his faults and his virtues for yourself?" A pause. "Do not look at me like that, Arthur. I am not fool enough to presume the fellow has no vices. Nor am I unkind enough to think him *entirely* vice. You have not met him, nor do you know him well enough to speak."

"I know his friends."

"Indeed you do! You are speaking to one of them."

"His London friends, father. A chap by the name of Lennox."

"George Lennox! By Providence, yes. We met the very fellow today. What a pity he did not get out of the carriage, for he might have greeted you this afternoon!"

There was no immediate response from her brother, and Amelia crept closer, almost cheering to find the door open a crack so that she could, if she positioned herself carefully, observe both gentlemen without herself being noticed.

Her brother had gone very quiet and was staring into the fire with a strange sort of intensity. Amelia frowned. Where was good-natured, light-hearted Arthur? And what had provoked such a change in his mood?

"It is a good job he did not, Father," Arthur muttered at last. "The fellow is a scoundrel. I did not like to say so within Milly's hearing, but -" He paused, before glancing over at her father so swiftly that Amelia, noticing the movement rather than the direction, took a hasty step backwards, melting into the darkness. She held her breath, but there was no indication that Arthur had seen her, or that her presence had been otherwise noticed, so she crept closer, once more, to the doorway.

"You speak of this Devereaux as a friend. You know as well as I that it is perfectly possible to be friends with a fellow whose morals are questionable on occasion." He smiled, grimly. "But you would not wish for such a fellow to marry your sister. Or daughter."

"Marry?" Admiral Sudbury chuckled as if the idea was nonsense, and Amelia felt a sharp prick of pain at her heart. Her own father thought the notion of Sir Benjamin Devereaux caring for her enough to consider marriage was ridiculous to the point of laughter! Yes, indeed! If he had encouraged her to welcome the gentleman it was surely only so that he, the admiral, might not feel uncomfortable about inviting his friend to their house whilst Amelia was present. He could not have thought of their having any sort of connection in and of themselves.

"No, no," Arthur chuckled in return. "You are quite right, it is a foolish proposition. Groundless. Poor Milly is far too sensible to form an affection for such a fellow."

Amelia bit her lip to keep from making a sound, and after a long moment, her father nodded, thoughtfully.

"Indeed, I think Amelia is safe from any involvement with such a gentleman." He relaxed, warming to his topic. "Yes, Arthur, if you wish to speak of the fellow's flaws I can think of no finer person to discuss them with than our Amelia. She has heard of Sir Benjamin's sins from his sister - oh, you did not meet Miss Devereaux yet, did you? She and her mother were quite alarmed at the sudden arrival of the late Sir Benjamin's estranged son. There was some scandal or other that sent him to London in the first place, and Amelia was adamant that his time abroad had nought but encouraged him along such a path of ignominy." He sighed. "Tis a pity, for he's an amusing fellow and a fine chess-player. I suppose we cannot all be saints, as you are."

Arthur snorted.

"I make no claims to piety, as well you know, Father. But I confess I like to think myself a damn sight more honourable than one who cheats at cards, as that weasel Lennox does, or runs amok with one's friends to such an extent that his reputation precedes him wherever he goes!"

Amelia could listen no longer. She felt her way carefully back to the bannister and retreated up the stairs to her bedroom. She was in no mood to read just then, feeling that no villain in a novel could possibly compare to the villain who had stolen her heart. What blackness and deceit to persuade her he was no villain at all, but merely misunderstood. A gentleman, yes, in word and deed as well as title. The victim of lies and misunderstanding his entire life. Why, she was a fool to have believed a word of it! Truly, Sir Benjamin Devereaux was nought but what she had thought him before they met, and she would not be so foolish as to believe a word that dripped from his honey lips ever again!

Chapter Seventeen

"'Twas only a few shillings." George Lennox screwed up his face in concentration as he tried in vain to summon up a name. "The fellow was named John, I believe. Or perhaps Samuel." He paused. "Smith. Or perhaps it was Wilkes. It is not always easy to hear in such places, and one is usually so bent on the game that one does not pause long to take down all the particulars of one's opponents." He stopped talking as a servant appeared, laying down a plate laden down with breakfast foods, and Lennox turned a simpering smile upon her. "You are very kind."

Devereaux did not smile but attended to the list he was taking based on Lennox's poor recollections. How was it possible that the fellow had left London less than three days prior and yet had already run up so many debts to so many strangers?

Lennox peered over at the note, tilting his head to one side so that he could read what Ben had written.

"You may discount above half the list," he commented, his words muffled over a mouthful of food. "I gave them my mark, they will be able to pursue it at their leisure."

"Or they will find it too arduous and abandon the attempt," Ben remarked, drily. "As was, no doubt, your intent."

Lennox smiled toothily at him. He appeared to think Devereaux's anger had been appeased, yet with every name he added to the list Ben merely grew more and more frustrated with his friend. Did Lennox care so little for the consequences of his actions, either for himself or his opponents? These were working men, many of them, spending money they could ill afford to lose and whilst he spared these men no sympathy for receiving unto themselves just punishment for their sins, he did object to Lennox profiting from their folly. He ought to know better, and, as a guest in this house, his poor behaviour was yet one more thing that would hinder Ben ever shaking off the mantel of rake that had fitted him so ill and yet clung so resolutely since his return to Westham.

"Very well, what is next? I feel certain we are not yet finished." He sighed. "Who did you play next, and what did you take from them?"

"You make me sound like a highwayman," Lennox protested. "It is not as if I stole from these men. They offered to play entirely of their own free will."

"And you applied no persuasion at all." Ben arched an eyebrow. "You did not throw a hand or two at first to suggest you were a poor player and encourage them to increase their bets, before suddenly rediscovering your skill?"

"I may have...managed their expectations of the game," Lennox conceded. He grinned, but one look at Ben's scowl wiped the expression from his face. "Very well. Heavens, Devereaux. I did not realise you left your sense of sport in London along with your friends."

"What friends?" Ben muttered. "I see only a problem I now need to resolve. I have enough strife of my own without your adding to it. Come, Lennox, who is next? I do not wish to devote longer than is necessary to repair the damage you caused."

George scowled, looking and acting like a young child who had been scolded for poor behaviour by a brother he scarcely considered his elder or better. Still, he complied, with a certain shyness that suggested he was not entirely insensible of his faults, nor of the impact they were likely to have on the man before him. He acknowledged, however grudgingly, that he was being shown hospitality he did not entirely deserve.

"Next?" He paused, taking a very sudden interest in straightening his unused cutlery. "Arthur Sudbury." This was little more than a whisper, but still, Ben heard it.

"Sudbury?" he asked, sharply. "Arthur Sudbury? Do you speak of Amelia - Miss Sudbury's brother? The admiral's son?" His heart sank. It was too ridiculous a coincidence to be true. Surely George mocked him, seeing a chance to redress the balance and have his own fun at Ben's expense.

"How was I to know the fellow was a friend of yours? It is not as if we traced one another's genealogies to the third generation!" Lennox was miserable, though, and pushed his plate back, his appetite gone. "It is why I was less than eager to vault from the carriage upon our arrival at the Sudbury's home," he confessed. "I did not put two and two together at first, thinking Sudbury a common enough name. That his father was an admiral was enough to give me pause, but I thought...I hoped..." He shook his head. "Damned fine card player, too. I almost regretted taking the money from him. He certainly made me earn it."

Ben felt a smile tug at his lips despite the absurd tragedy of the situation. His friend had scammed Amelia's brother from a small fortune. However, could he convince them not to hold it against him? Admiral Sudbury, perhaps, might see the matter as a gentlemanly dispute, particularly once reparations were made and debts repaid, but Amelia? She would see it as proof that Devereaux was a rake, with rakish friends and that all his protestations to the contrary were falsehoods designed to persuade her of that which was not true.

"Come, Lennox." He sighed, massaging his forehead. "Let us go now and visit the captain. He is the nearest on this list and the first we might resolve." He did not say *the easiest*. There would be nothing easy about apologising to one set of friends over the actions of another. He could already imagine the cold glance Amelia would turn on him. It would be the end of his trying, in spite of himself, to win her heart. *Perhaps it is what I need,* he thought. *I have allowed myself the dream of her for far too long. Some reputations are too ingrained to ever be overcome, and even if they are not true to begin with does not mean they do not become true over time.*

Wearily, feeling as if he had a world of weight pressing down on his shoulders, he got to his feet.

Lennox, at least, seemed a little revived by his meal and the promise of a plan to execute. He smiled almost cheerfully and whilst this ought to have angered Ben still more he could not help but feel his irritation towards his friend fading as they made their way towards Devereaux's carriage. Lennox was Lennox, be he in London or elsewhere. He might claim a need to change, but until he wished it for himself, it would be nought but an instrument to manipulate those closest to him.

"You'll go on from here this afternoon, then?" It was a question, but he scarcely expected a response. Lennox, to his surprise, nodded meekly, a picture of contrition.

"I have an aunt in Brighton," he said. "I am long overdue a visit to her, kind lady, and I shall seek to remedy my follies there." His eyes sparkled. "I do appreciate this, Dev, though I know I do not seem as if I do. I am a mess and undeserving of such a friend."

Ben tried to maintain his anger, but he could not help the scowl slipping from his face at this frank, self-deprecating admission.

"You ought to seek better friends," he growled, as the two men settled into the carriage. "I think my helping you does not, truly, help you, and that is my own cross to bear. Seek better society, Lennox, quieter society, and see if you do not find the means to motivate you towards change." His thoughts strayed to Amelia, and he treasured this last glimpse of her while she still might care for him. After the interview to come, she would loathe him and he was not quite ready yet to let go of the dream of her, whatever he told himself.

❧

"AMELIA, DEAR..." ADMIRAL Sudbury's voice was gentle, his words laden with concern. "Is anything the matter?"

"The matter?" Amelia was breathless with exertion. She paused for a moment as she passed her father's study and stepped inside. "Why do you ask?"

"That is the fourth time this morning you have passed by the door of my study with your arms laden with books." He pointed at the cloth-bound volumes she hugged to her chest. "Are you reorganising your small library?"

"Not reorganising." Amelia dropped the pile of books onto her father's desk with a thump. "Deconstructing. Discarding. Doing away with."

The admiral's bushy eyebrows lifted quite enthusiastically.

"Indeed? Whatever for? You treasure your bookshelves and their contents. Why all of a sudden do you wish to be rid of the possessions it has taken you half your lifetime to accumulate, and which bring you such joy?"

"*Brought* me such joy," Amelia corrected. She wiped her dusty hands on the front of her dress and wondered, fleetingly, if she ought to have worn an apron. Her mania for destruction had come upon her all of a sudden and before she had time to consider her apparel she had launched into her task. Her books had been her most treasured possessions, yes, close confidants and companions during many long, quiet hours at home while her father was otherwise occupied. But they had betrayed her! They had told her that villains could be redeemed, that true love was enough to turn even the blackest heart pure, that any heroine, no matter how mousy or unremarkable, would be seen as beautiful and desirable by the man she truly loved. All of these were fabrications and had been proved to be so by her short, tumultuous acquaintance with Sir Benjamin Devereaux. There would be no escaping him, alas, for he seemed poised to stay at home at Roland Park for the foreseeable future. But Amelia could get rid of the novels that had caused her to see him as anything other than what he was: her neighbour, her father's friend, and entirely unsuitable for her to set her heart upon.

"These novels have led me astray, Papa, they have caused me to think things that are not true." Amelia slumped into a chair. "And I do not wish to be so silly again, so I will bid them farewell. It is as Mr Connelly said at breakfast that day, novels encourage foolishness. Far better I focus my reading on things that will improve my character, rather than inflaming my imagination."

Admiral Sudbury said nothing but continued to regard his daughter in curious silence. Amelia knew this trick of her father's well and still, she seemed to fall for it whenever it was deployed. Almost before she was conscious of it she felt her lips part and she began to speak again.

"I know you will think I am overreacting, and perhaps I am, but -"

She stopped herself just in time. Although she and her father had always been close, perhaps even more so since the loss of her mother and Arthur's absence, but even so there were certain things a young lady did not naturally care to speak of with her father.

A knock at the door saved her having to explain further, and she straightened as Arthur stepped into the room.

"What cosy meeting of minds is going on in here, then?" He grinned, ducking his head so that his tall frame could fit through the doorway. "I am almost sorry to break it up. And yet! Father, it appears you have guests." His features drew into a grimace. "At least one of them I do not trust myself to treat with civility, so I implore you to greet them with me and I will attempt to remind myself I am no longer on board a ship, where a minor disagreement is better resolved with my fists than my words."

Amelia might have been shocked to hear such words from good-natured, kind-hearted Arthur, had they not been followed by a hearty wink.

"Shall I come too?" she asked both gentleman's retreating backs and not knowing which answer she would prefer.

In the end, she could restrain her curiosity no longer. She waited until she heard the front door open and two sets of heavy masculine footsteps follow their housekeeper into the parlour. Taking a deep breath, she peered out into the corridor, and, finding it empty, crept along it on tiptoes, hesitating by the half-open parlour door.

If I can but see him once more... she thought. Then, *No, I cannot. I do not wish ever to set eyes on him again, the deceitful, cruel, monstrous -*

"Amelia?"

Admiral Sudbury's voice rang with amusement but it was too late. Almost before she was conscious of it, her traitorous feet propelled her forwards and she pushed the door open wide enough to permit her entrance.

"Miss Sudbury, good afternoon." The gentleman who greeted her was not Sir Benjamin but his friend, who shielded his eyes with one hand as if the brightness of the room hurt him. His voice was gravelly and thick, not at all the same fellow she recalled meeting in town, but she obediently curtseyed and made her way swiftly to a chair, not quite trusting her eyes to rest on Devereaux for more than the briefest moment. Even that was too much, for he looked at her with such affection and such longing that for a moment she was pinned in place.

"Do you intend to haunt the doorway, Milly? Come, sit by me and help your brother to mind his words now that he is a gentleman amongst other gentlemen." Arthur placed heavy emphasis on the word *gentlemen* and a ripple of uncomfortable laughter echoed around the room. Amelia glanced around her in confusion, but in the end her brother's was the only suggestion that offered her the chance to hide, for the chair he pointed to was a high wing-back seat and Amelia sank gratefully into it, glad to be hidden a little from the scrutiny she had felt in the doorway of the room. Still, she was opposite Devereaux, and no chair in their house could have hidden her from the piercing gaze he rested on her. Despite her intentions to hold fast against him, she could not help but read some question in his eyes, some hesitancy as he looked at her. This was not Sir Benjamin Devereaux, the irredeemable rake who she had been foolish to believe in, this was Benjamin, the gentleman who brought her a bookmark and teased her as if they had known each other far longer than mere weeks. She ducked her gaze, certain that her features would betray her if she allowed him to look upon them any longer. This was Benjamin, the man she loved, in spite of all that she knew, or thought she knew, about him. When he looked at her like that, with something that looked like love in his eyes, she dared to think he might care for her too.

Chapter Eighteen

Devereaux was staring. He shifted in his seat, forcing his gaze away from Amelia and focusing it on something, anything else The fire. The mantelpiece. His shoes. The Admiral. The admiral's daughter. Catching his breath, he swallowed and attempted to draw Arthur into a conversation. Anything to distract himself from the picture of prettiness that sat at Arthur's left hand. He had seen beautiful women before, women who society would suggest were far more beautiful than delicate Amelia Sudbury, yet Ben had never known his attention and imagination to be captured so completely by any one of them.

"How long do you intend to remain at home, Captain Sudbury?" he asked, finding, at last, a satisfactory topic of discussion.

"My time is my own for the present," Arthur replied, with a tight, fixed smile. It was a smile that said, *I will answer you to be polite, but had I free reign I would not choose to speak to you at all.* He lifted his head, nodding towards Lennox. "And you, sir? How long will you be staying at Roland Place?" Again, Ben fancied he knew the questions Arthur had truly wished he was able to ask. *How long will you outstay your welcome? How long will you exploit your connection to my father's newest neighbour? How long must we endure being pressed into society together?*

"Actually, Mr Lennox will bid us farewell as early as this afternoon."

Poor Lennox flushed a little, and Ben began to feel a growing sympathy for his friend. Had he expected too much too soon? He knew people spoke of gambling as a monster that was not easily shaken. Lennox had been alone and vulnerable, travelling through places he did not know to a friend he only hoped would welcome him, as he had done too many times in London, without reprimand. Ben sighed, wondering if his defence of his friends had been complicity. It had been within his power to counsel them to change. At first, he had revelled in the opportunity to befriend those his father would despair of, thinking he was in some way getting back at the man who had exiled him from his home. He saw now that he had played his own part in inflaming the rumours that were spread about him. How likely would people have been to believe Lady Devereaux's account over his if his life had been demonstrably blameless ever since? A low groan sounded in his throat and he realised, with dismay, the sound had carried to the ears of at least one of his companions.

"Is something the matter, Devereaux?" Arthur's eyes were sharp.

Amelia straightened in her seat, the movement catching Ben's eye. He well knew what was the matter with him. Too much repentance, too late, and regret that by virtue of his friends he would forever be judged and found wanting. But Amelia? What could plague her so that she kept her gaze continually, painfully, averted from his? Concern knit his brows.

"You are very quiet, Miss Sudbury, I hope you do not find your peace intruded upon by myself or my friend. Forgive us, we may take our leave if you prefer -"

"No!" Amelia smiled, but the expression was desperate, rather than welcoming. "That is, you are welcome to stay as long as you wish to. I think - I think I am a little tired, though, and may bid you farewell."

She stood, and to Ben's disappointment, swept towards the door.

"Do not forget those books you left in my study, dear," Admiral Sudbury murmured, as she passed his chair. "I know you claim you want rid of them but I dare say you will change your mind. I shall keep them for you until the end of the day and I suggest you do not let them go without one more examination."

This caught Ben's ear and he frowned. Amelia was discarding her books? Yet, had her affection for reading not been almost the first detail he had come to know about his new friend?

She had escaped before she could be questioned on this or anything else, so Ben applied himself to her father.

"I hope there is no problem with Miss Sudbury's library?"

"Ha!" Admiral Sudbury shook his head. "She is talking of ridding herself of her books." He waved his hand in dismissal. "There is some reason far too convoluted for any one of us to fully understand, I am sure." His eyes met Arthur's and the two men smiled, looking more alike than Ben had noticed upon their first meeting.

"Poor Milly lives too often in the pages of her books," Arthur remarked, and then, as if recalling he was not speaking to his father alone, he fixed a blank stare on Devereaux. "She ought to remember that life is not a story, and not every villain can be easily redeemed within a few pages."

Something about Arthur's imperious tone rattled Ben, reminding him of his stepmother. He might dismiss Ben on first acquaintance, as had much of Westham, but that did not mean Ben was left without redress.

"Yet, Captain, I humbly suggest that stories allow us to believe that villains might be afforded the opportunity to change." He smiled, grimly. "I concede to your point that it may take longer than a chapter, but in the end, redemption is possible for us all, or else why keep trying?"

Arthur's features transformed as if he was surprised to hear such philosophy from the lips of a man he had been poised to dislike. He smiled, almost in spite of himself, and smacked his knee.

"I'm damned if you are not right, Father. This fellow is clever, far cleverer than many bestowed with the title of *sir*."

Admiral Sudbury laughed, but Ben thought he detected a glimmer of anxiety as the old man darted a glance towards his guest. He smiled, to show that he was not offended by Arthur's blunt observation. In fact, he felt as if he rather preferred the young man for his honesty. It would mean more to win the respect of a man such as Captain Arthur Sudbury, particularly when the odds were stacked against his success in ever doing so.

He settled back into his seat, allowing his thoughts to stray. He was fond of this family, already, and felt privileged to have won, or begun winning, the admiration and friendship of father and son. If only Amelia was not such a confusion to him! He could make no decision upon her feelings towards him.

He knew what he hoped them to be, yes, and what he did not deserve them to be! Yet, when she had looked at him just then her eyes had been so filled with something...hope? Yes, hope. It had taken all his strength not to eschew the stares of the other gentlemen present and speak plainly to her then and there. But that would be too rude, too shocking, and he determined that he would do all he could to protect Amelia from ever enduring such scandal. He would be patient, for, in that glance, she had encouraged him he had a reason to be. She might love him, she might not, but he would not give up hope quite yet that the matter was resolved. A slow smile crept onto his features. There was the assembly to come, after all, and if there was one element of society he was well versed in it was the business of assemblies.

⊙≫✦≪⊚

"AMELIA?"

Some days had passed since the last time Amelia had been hailed from within her father's study. Days where they had had nary a visitor, for Devereaux had not set foot on their doorstep since, which fact nettled Amelia more than she cared to admit.

"Papa." She smiled as he beckoned her across the threshold and into the comfort of his room. "Are you alone?"

"Yes, alone and undisturbed." He grimaced. "Come and disturb me a little bit. Do you know, I felt certain that when your brother came home I would have far less time to myself." His grimace relaxed into a smile. "It seems I was mistaken, for Arthur is scarcely here but to sleep. It seems he has found himself a firm friend in Sir Benjamin and has forsaken our company for his almost entirely!" He laughed, but Amelia felt that she detected a glimmer of disappointment in her father's weathered features.

"Not to worry, Papa," She said, sliding into the seat opposite him and enfolding one of his large hands in both of hers. "You have me still, and likely will forever." Her smile fell a little, though she strove not to let him notice. "I do not think I shall ever have cause to leave here."

Instead of lifting his mood, though, this seemed merely to worsen it, and his features drew down still further into a grimace, and Amelia hurried to forestall what he must surely be about to suggest.

"I do not mind it, Father, so please do not try your hand at matchmaking any more, for I am sorry to tell you...you are not very good at it."

The admiral's eyebrows lifted, and he looked at his daughter askance.

"Matchmaking? Whatever can you mean?"

"Mr Connelly," Amelia said patiently. "I am no fool, Father, and it was plain from the start why you sought to pursue such a friendship with so unlikely a fellow."

Bristling, the admiral shook his head.

"I sought a friendship with Sir Benjamin Devereaux, too, my dear. Do you think I did that purely for your benefit?"

Amelia coloured. If anything, her father's friendship with Benjamin Devereaux had been to Amelia's detriment but she was not about to admit as much to the admiral, for fear he felt himself due to lose yet another of his offspring to Devereaux's inner circle.

"But I confess, I may have considered the curate a sensible option for you, at least I considered him so. You would be cleverer than him, naturally, but as your mother was far cleverer than I, I saw no problem in that. The poor man would need to lose a little of his piety though, if he were to truly be acceptable as a son-in-law." His eyes twinkled. "You are sure you will not be convinced to consider him?"

Amelia shook her head, emphatically.

"I would rather be a spinster all my days." The words had never seemed so grim and uninspiring as they did upon that utterance. *Of course, before Sir Benjamin, there was no man I should care to marry instead, so that marriage could be preferable to spinsterhood.* She tried to inject her voice with a brightness she did not feel. "I shall keep house for you, Papa, and for Arthur until he finds a wife of his own."

Admiral Sudbury did not answer in words but Amelia felt, from the slight nod he gave as the only indication he had heard her, that he was not entirely satisfied by this answer.

The door opened and Arthur crashed through the house, forestalling any further discussion.

"Father! What are you doing holed up in here? The weather is delightful outside. Devereaux and I intend on walking to town, and he bade me come and see if you care to join us. Oh, Milly!" he exclaimed, almost tripping over his sister. "Well, you can come too, I suppose. I expect Miss Devereaux might be persuaded to join us if you will come. What a jolly party we shall make. You'll come, Father?"

"I certainly shall!" Admiral Sudbury was hurrying to his feet, stopped only by the anxious expression in his daughter's eyes as he reached for his cane. "That is, I shall walk a little way with you. I do not know if these old sea legs will permit me to walk all the way to town, but I daresay I can manage part of the journey, at least."

"Excellent! Come, hurry and get ready. I told Devereaux we would meet him at the fork in the road in a quarter-hour."

He had retreated back out of the study almost as quickly as he had entered it, in a flurry of preparation and Amelia turned to her father with the ghost of a frown hovering over her features.

"You are sure you shall manage the walk, Papa?" she asked.

"Indeed I shall!" Admiral Sudbury bristled. "I shall manage many other things besides, my dear, just you wait and see. Now, be a gem and run down to the kitchen. See if the cook can't spare us a heel of bread and a few slices of fruit cake, for if we are to undertake this expedition, we must ensure the troops are properly fed, mustn't we?" His eyes twinkled with merriment and he looked more like his old self. Amelia dropped a kiss on his thin cheek, and flew to her task, absently brushing down her dress and wishing she possessed another that would be suitable for walking in that certain members of their party had not already had cause to see her wearing so often.

"Oh, Milly, before you go," Admiral Sudbury called. Amelia paused in the doorway and turned back to see him holding out an armful of books.

"You deposited these here almost a week ago, now, and I am loathe to dispose of them, feeling certain you would change your mind." He smiled. "*Udolpho?* You will cast him aside, too? And what of *The Wicked Rake?* Surely you still have a little room in your heart for him?"

He chuckled, amused by the sentence as he held the books out to her. Blushing, although her father could not have intended his words to spark her thoughts in the direction that they did, she reached for the books.

"Do not dispose of your books entirely, my dear. They have given you such joy, and what is life without a little adventure, albeit consigned to the page?" His eyes sparkled. "Who knows but that life can sometimes learn to imitate art?"

Amelia frowned, wondering, then, if her father was quite aware of his words. Indeed, whether he chose them precisely for the thoughts they might provoke in her. She nodded, holding the books close to her heart and turning back to her task. Life might imitate art, but hers ought not to. Was it not the fault of these books that she had lost her heart to Devereaux, to begin with? Her eyes fell to the cover, and she swallowed. They had ignited her affection for him, yes. Perhaps they would be just the thing to quell it, too. Lifting *The Wicked Rake*, she slipped the small cloth-bound book into her reticule, as if holding it close would allow it to be a talisman, protecting her against a wicked rake of her own, reminding her just who Devereaux was, and why the idea of loving him at all, or him loving her, was so utterly impossible.

Chapter Nineteen

Devereaux waited with Joanna at the fork in the road that was the meeting place he had agreed with Arthur Sudbury half an hour earlier. He was a little surprised that his sister had agreed to join them, not thinking her fond of long walks or of him, but a strange silence had pervaded the air at Roland Park when he entered it, and he found that both his sister and stepmother were in no humour to be left together. They seemed to be ignoring one another, and he fleetingly considered that he might somehow be the cause of this antagonism. He dismissed the thought almost immediately, however, for, whilst relations seemed to be improving with his sister, his stepmother still refused to speak more than mere civilities to him. Even those had been lessened over the most recent days, for she had been attending with ever more fervour to her correspondence. Letters flew from and to her with such regularity that, had Ben a suspicious nature, he might have thought her planning some sort of coup. The answer was on Joanna's lips before he had even formulated the question.

"You know Mama intends to leave us?"

They had been standing in silence, waiting for their friends to join them. Joanna's words were uttered so matter-of-factly, apropos of nothing, that Ben turned to look at her, frowning in surprise and confusion.

"How do you know that?"

"She told me." Joanna pulled her wrap closer, lifting her chin and fixing him with a defiant stare. "When I asked her to tell me the truth about why you left. Or," Her gaze faltered, her voice dropping to little more than a whisper. "Why *she made you leave.*" She frowned. "I had no idea anyone could be so unkind, and to have the audacity to remain in your home - for Roland Park is yours now, whatever she might wish. She told me she has no intention of remaining where she is not wanted and was merely using this time to make such plans as would settle her comfortably elsewhere before you revealed your true intentions towards us and had us cast out."

Now, he saw the reason for her question, as her gaze falteringly settled upon him again. "You will not make us *both* leave, will you, Ben?"

He might have given any one of a hundred responses, but he saw the sister he had loved and lost in those features, the slightly hopeful turn of her eyes, the lips that trembled a little as they spoke.

"No, Josie. I will not make you *both* leave."

A smile - the first real, genuine smile he had won from her since his return - began to creep onto Joanna's face and she looked for a moment as if she was about to embrace him. Instead, she offered a hand that he, stiffly, shook. He wondered if ever they would overcome the awkwardness of their separation, and decided that this first, frank conversation was the beginning.

"I am sorry," Joanna whispered, as he let go of her hand. "I believed what she said about you. All these years I have been so angry about what you did, and - and how it affected us."

She smiled, self-deprecatingly. "I can be terribly selfish at times, Benjamin, as I am sure Amelia will attest -"

"Amelia is your friend," he said, reflexively. "What makes you think she would be anything other than complimentary? Especially within my hearing?" He did not say, *lately, I am lucky if she speaks to me at all,* but something in his gaze or his voice must have betrayed him because Joanna's smile grew.

"She may be my friend, but it would not surprise me if you are the one she truly cares to know," Joanna remarked. "Ah, look, you may discover for yourself: they are coming." She raised her hand to wave a greeting to their friends, and Ben followed suit, struggling to order his thoughts, which had all sprung to attention after these surprising words from his sister. Did Amelia care to know him? Did he dare to think such a thing possible?

"Here we are, Devereaux!" Arthur called, cheerfully. "Forgive us, did we keep you waiting?"

"Not at all." Ben bowed, his eyes lighting first on Amelia and then her father. "Admiral Sudbury! I am so glad you could join us. And Miss Sudbury. You are content to walk to town with us? I hope it is not too far."

"Sir Benjamin, when we first we met I had walked to town and back," Amelia said, with a mischievous smile. "But perhaps you forget."

His smile grew.

"How could I forget such a meeting?"

Arthur Sudbury cleared his throat, and Ben, forestalling his teasing or censure, turned back to his sister.

"Well, shall we begin? Let us make the most of this good weather while it remains."

The party began to walk. They made a merry group, for their pace was leisurely, yet brisk, and the sky shone with pleasant winter sunshine.

"I hope you intend to join us at the upcoming assembly, Captain Sudbury," Joanna called, disentangling herself from her own brother's arm so that she might address Amelia's. Ben was left to walk alone and found himself slowing, matching his pace to Admiral Sudbury's, while the two young ladies and Arthur discussed, in detail, their plans for the upcoming ball. Ben's ears were pricked to their conversation, but he did not wish to be seen eavesdropping and opened a conversation with the admiral.

"I trust you are adjusting to having a rather fuller household than you have had for some time," he remarked, with a cheerful smile.

"Indeed!" Admiral Sudbury laughed. "And yet, Arthur is so often out of doors that we scarcely notice a difference. I trust he is not making a nuisance of himself."

"I see him even less than you do!" Ben acknowledged, with a frown. "I thought he kept mostly to home, to spend time with the family he has been so long apart from."

Admiral Sudbury knit his brows, shooting a curious look at his son's back.

"I expect he is enjoying the freedom to explore, and I dare say he has many other friends hereabouts," Ben said, quickly, wishing to allay the admiral's concerns. He made a mental note to extract the truth from Arthur when he next had the chance, for Admiral Sudbury had spoken with such certainty that he felt as if his own name had been offered as an alibi far more than it ought to have. He must remind his young friend what troubles came of untruth before damage was done to a family he had come to care for as if they were his own. His eyes strayed to Amelia, who looked with such reverence towards her brother that his own heart constricted. He could not bear her being hurt by her brother's behaviour, whatever it was. He knew only too well the damage such deception could do to relations between a brother and a sister.

There was a style ahead to cross and the party slowed, as Arthur clambered over, reaching back a hand for Joanna. Amelia ought to have been next, but she caught her dress on a bramble and stopped to free it. Admiral Sudbury climbed over the style next, needing but refusing to take any assistance. Ben stood back, watching to be sure that he could step in to help his friend if needed, but at last, the admiral's feet were firmly on the ground once more.

"Miss Sudbury," he called, at last, as the first half of their party continued walking and the distance between them grew. "You must allow me to help you continue on our path."

Amelia nodded, hurrying up to the style. Ben held her hand lightly in his, wondering if, even through gloves, she felt the jolt that passed between them. She turned to look at him, then, and missed her footing. Quick as a flash, Devereaux reached up to secure her, and she was saved. Her reticule, alas, was not, and it tumbled to the ground, dropping its contents into the dirt.

"Oh!" Amelia cried, bending to retrieve it. Ben reached for the book, slower this time, but more insistent as his hands closed around the slim volume. Amelia relinquished her hold on it as if the book were aflame, and had burned her. Ben's eyes fell on the title and a sly smile crept onto his lips.

"Miss Sudbury!" he exclaimed, his tone warm with the affection he was tired of concealing. "You are reading, still. I wonder that you do not feel you have far too many dealings with wicked rakes already that you need to seek them out in literature."

Amelia reached for the book again but he held it aloft.

"A moment, Miss Sudbury, for I must study the form if I am to embody it accurately." He patted his chest. "I am already dressed the part, I think, in swirling black coat, and hat, and scowl." He forced his features to smile no longer. "Yes, that part I have great success at. A mysterious past, too. Well, I am already aware of your acquaintance with my past misdeeds." His smile cracked. "I wonder what it means for the noble rake if they are proven false?"

"They are?" Amelia's voice was little more than a whisper, heavy with hope, and when her gaze met his, Ben dropped his charade and grew serious once more.

"They are. But I am not. Miss Sudbury, I know that our acquaintance has been underpinned by suspicion and rumour, but now I stand before you as I truly am. All pretence aside. I am no rake, although I have certainly lived my share of mistakes." He blinked, but his gaze did not falter. "The worst of which was not telling you, the first moment I met you, how much I admired you. That admiration has merely grown with our acquaintance. I - I love you, Miss Sudbury." He swallowed. "Amelia. I know it is foolish to ask that you return my feelings, but I dare to hope that one day you might. Am I mistaken?"

AMELIA'S THROAT HAD constricted so much that she was not capable of speaking a word at first. She swallowed, opening her mouth at last and forcing herself to make some sound if only to convince herself that she was still alive, that all this was truly happening, and not merely a dream.

"No. Yes. I mean –" She was stammering, watching Devereaux's reactions and trying, quickly, to remedy them. She took a breath, glancing up towards the heavens as if seeking some assistance. When her lips parted again she managed to speak only a few words, but so succinctly and honestly that both her heart and Devereaux's were put at ease.

"You are not mistaken," she murmured, finding she was able only to look at Benjamin or to speak, not both. She dropped her eyes to the ground, to the foot or so of space between them, and found herself able to continue. "I ought not to talk of love –"

"Then don't," Benjamin said, swiftly taking a step closer to her. Instinctively, Amelia moved back. The movement forced her eyes upwards and she saw he wore a smile, gentler and more welcoming than any she had seen him wear before. "And I shall not either. We might be friends, at least?"

There was such hope in this, such simplicity, that Amelia wished she could say yes. She knew, though, that she could never merely be friends with Benjamin Devereaux. She bit her lip and his smile faltered before she took a breath and tried again to speak.

"I ought not to talk of love," she said again, haltingly. "Because it is improper and because it is so unlikely as to end in my making a fool of myself. But as you have spoken of it first..." She took a breath. "It is up to me to be as brave as I can be. Sir Benjamin, I have spent the last weeks listing every reason I could conjure why I shouldn't care for you. My mind denounced it as foolishness, but my heart refused to listen. I blamed my books for fuelling my imagination, but perhaps it is good they did, for there is no logic to our caring for one another and yet...I do. I do care for you, very much."

There was silence following this little speech so that Amelia was briefly uncertain whether she had even spoken it aloud, or merely thought it.

"Sir Benjamin?" Her eyes searched his face.

"Do not call me *Sir Benjamin* as if we are strangers, Amelia," Devereaux said, gently.

"Then what am I to call you?" She laughed, and all at once the anxiety that had kept them rigidly apart receded. "I shall not call you *Devereaux* as my brother does, nor *Dev* like Mr Lennox." She wrinkled her nose. "Both make you sound so..." She threw up her hands. "Rakish."

"And *Sir Benjamin* recalls me to my father," he said, glowering fiercely and looking, momentarily, the very picture of the villain he had claimed to be. Amelia blinked, and the picture shifted.

"You are not your father," she said, softly. "You are entirely yourself." Shyly, she tried the name she had heard Joanna call him but once when she forgot herself in a moment of familiarity that bordered on affection. She was not affectionate, but the name was, and on Amelia's lips it sounded the very dearest word of all. "Ben."

This prompted a smile, the same warm, gentle, endearing expression that she had seen only glimpses of before. This was *Ben*, and there was no cynicism, no manipulation, no anything but sincerity and love. Amelia smiled back, and this time, when he moved closer to her she did not move away.

"Then we are agreed, Amelia?" His voice was little more than a whisper, but he was so close that she could feel the warmth of his breath on her cheek. "Logic or no, we have found one another, and we might, somehow, be happy together?"

He held his hand out to her, this time not to help her over a style nor to give her anything but the promise of his heart and a future by his side. For the first time with absolute confidence, Amelia laid her hand in his, meeting his gaze and smiling as he leaned closer to kiss her.

"Yes, Ben, we are agreed," she murmured, their faces inches apart. "And I think we might manage to be very happy together."

Chapter Twenty

They had walked on several paces before Joanna Devereaux noticed the absence of Amelia, and not only her friend but her brother, also. She stopped, peering back over her shoulder and saw the pair frozen in what appeared to be a very serious conversation. Fearing that to draw attention to it would be to ruin the moment, and feeling a flicker of hope that this was the very moment she had lately been praying for, where her brother and her friend - who she had once vowed to forever keep apart - might, at last, be given the opportunity to acknowledge how well they might suit one another, she averted her gaze almost immediately.

"I wonder, Miss Devereaux, at you and my sister regularly making such a journey on foot. I trust you are not over-exerting yourself to maintain our pace. Perhaps you would care to rest awhile..."

Captain Sudbury began to look around for a tree stump or low wall which might serve as an impromptu bench and Joanna, fearing his gaze would fall on the couple and prompt him to interrupt what, she felt sure, must be a declaration of affection, she hurried to distract him.

"Oh, I am quite alright, Captain Sudbury. You give us ladies little credit for our energy. How much do you think it requires to dance a full evening at an assembly, in shoes far less comfortable than your boots?" She smiled, widely, and was pleased to see him return it, acknowledging with a sheepish nod that he was, indeed, quick to judge and ought to know better, being in possession of a sister who reminded him all too often that young ladies were no different from the gentlemen counterparts and in no greater need of handling with kid gloves.

"Where has Amelia got to?" the admiral murmured, and Joanna seized on something – anything – that might keep both her companions' attention fixed on her and their present occupation, and allow Amelia and her brother a few moments more without interruption.

"Oh, look! A bird! What kind is that, do you think?" She pointed, and both gentlemen obediently looked into the sky.

"That?" Arthur's voice rang with restrained laughter. "Why, I believe it is a blackbird, Miss Devereaux. Are you not well-acquainted with such a common species?"

"Oh!" Joanna laughed. "Of course, I did not mean *that* bird. But its companion. Look, that smaller one, with the brownish feathers."

"A starling."

Joanna opened her mouth, but Arthur forestalled her.

"And that, there, with the fascinating redbreast, is a robin, unless I am very much mistaken." He raised his eyebrows. "No, Miss Devereaux, you pointed out quite rightly that I ought not to consider women feebler in body than men when it comes to walking, I plead with you not to do the same with men's minds, for you shall not convince me we are less clever than ladies. My astronomy is better than my ornithology, I'll grant you, but still

-" He paused, glancing up as the rest of their party hurried to join them.

"Here you are, Devereaux. We wondered if you had got yourself lost!" His eyebrows lifted as his gaze reached his sister. "Did you keep the poor fellow waiting, Milly? How hard can it be to clamber over a style?"

"Actually -" Amelia was flushed, her eyes darting from one member of their party before they rested, anxiously, on Joanna. She felt a little surprised to find that the person whose opinion Amelia most feared hearing was hers as if she could ever be anything other than truly happy that her friend and her brother might find happiness together. She remembered, with a sick feeling in her stomach, that the last time she and Amelia had spoken of Devereaux it had not been in complimentary terms, and it was likely that this was precisely what Amelia feared. Joanna, despising her brother, would likewise despise her friend for choosing him. She smiled, hoping to convey in the guileless expression that this thought could not be further from the truth.

"Admiral Sudbury, Captain Sudbury." It was Ben who spoke, so quietly and with such formality that all trace of humour slipped from the other gentlemen's features.

"Is something the matter?" the admiral asked, momentarily alarmed. His eyes slid to his daughter, and then back to Benjamin.

"No." Ben smiled, the first broad, genuine smile Joanna had seen him wear in a decade. He looked younger, then, more like the brother she remembered from her childhood, and she wondered how she could have believed him capable of the dreadful things she had held against him for so long. This was her brother, her own Ben, and he had found love with her best friend! It could not be more perfect had she orchestrated it herself, instead of longing to prevent it.

"Captain Sudbury, you claim that your skill at ornithology is lacking, yet I am sure it is far better than mine. Might I persuade you to help me to identify this particular creature?"

She could tell, by Arthur's posture, that he was disinclined to move away from their party, wanting, no doubt, to hear what Devereaux wished to say. Of the two gentlemen in Amelia's life, however, Joanna thought he was the most likely to disapprove, and sought to give her brother the opportunity to win the acceptance of the older Sudbury before he tried the younger. With a vaguely resigned sigh, Arthur agreed, and the two of them stepped away.

"There is mischief afoot, Miss Devereaux, and you must think me a fool indeed not to notice," he grumbled, as soon as they were out of earshot of the rest of their party. Joanna glanced up at him, momentarily fearful until she saw the sparkle in his eyes, so like, and yet so unlike, his sister's.

"I dare say you know the truth of it, so speak, do, and put me out of my misery. I never could bear to enduring suspense."

"Captain Sudbury!" Joanna adopted a cautionary tone. "Were you not the gentleman who, not five minutes ago, declared that men were no less intelligent than ladies? Examine the evidence, then, and tell me what conclusion anyone with even the merest hint of intelligence must draw."

He glanced back at the three, saw the broad smile break out on his father's features, mirrored on Devereaux's and Amelia's faces, and groaned.

"There is to be a wedding, I suppose!"

"Well!" Joanna laughed. "You need not sound so happy about it."

"I am," he growled. "That is, I shall be." He looked down at his feet, digging a groove in the dirt with the toe of one boot. "Miss Devereaux, I do not expect you to understand this, but I have not seen my sister in many years. Is it selfish of me to struggle to realise she is grown into a young woman capable of marriage? I wished her to be my baby sister, still, for everything to remain as it was."

"You despise change." Joanna arched an eyebrow. "You wish to have all the adventures yourself, and leave the rest of us mired in the endless nothing of the countryside."

A smile crept onto Arthur's features and grew until he hooted with laughter.

"I see why my sister is such good friends with you, Miss Devereaux. You possess the same skill of presenting a fellow's shortcomings to him, and not giving him an ounce of sympathy when he is being ridiculous." He shook himself. "Yes, I suppose you are right. I have had my adventures. Why not allow my sister a few of her own?"

But as his gaze returned to the small, rejoicing party, Joanna thought she noticed a cloud flit over his handsome features. Before she could inquire as to its meaning, or contemplate it further, however, Admiral Sudbury called over to alert them to the news.

"Our Milly, Arthur!" he beamed. "And Sir Benjamin Devereaux! Why, 'tis a better match than even I could have wished for. I think we must make our way to town in double quick time so that we might celebrate with a drink. What say you?"

"DO YOU REGRET US ANNOUNCING it so soon?" Ben asked, when he had at last freed his hand from being heartily shaken by Amelia's father and brother, and father again.

She smiled, leaning closer to him as they walked, surprised to feel so at ease with the gentleman she had scarcely dared to look at only days earlier. Her nerves had vanished, chased away with the simple knowledge that he cared for her as she did him. It still seemed unreal to her, and she admitted as much.

"I can scarcely believe it is true!" She smiled. "I dare say it will serve me well that my brother and father can remind me today actually happened, for I am sure to think I dreamt it when I wake up tomorrow.

"T'would be a dream, then?" Devereaux asked, his eyes sparkling with fun. "Not a nightmare? To find oneself engaged to be married to *Devereaux the Rake*."

"You give yourself rather too much of a reputation, sir," Amelia said, jabbing him in the side. "You may have been the victim of rumour and speculation, but you certainly did not deserve a name like that." She raised her eyebrows. "Although I dare say it suits you."

He affected the pose of a fashion plate, frowning in a manner of great villainy.

Amelia laughed, and Ben looked so crestfallen that she immediately repented.

"I apologise. But if you were ever so very terrifying, do you really think I could have come to care for you?"

"I think you are capable of caring for even the most villainous wretch," he said, valiantly. "Far worse than me. You deserve far better."

"There is none," Amelia said, simply. "I still cannot believe you would choose me, who has lived so little and been nowhere of any great interest." Her heart constricted. "I have heard you and my brother talking, and my father, too, about the places you have visited, about politics and the war and all sorts of things I do not know." She tried to keep the fear from sounding in her voice that soon, very soon, Ben would wake up and realise he had made a mistake. Surely he could not truly be happy with her?

"Just because I have travelled means I wish to continue it." Ben slowed his pace, forcing her to look at him. "Even your brother, I fancy, is weary of adventuring. See how eager he is to be at home, at last? And society!" Ben snorted. "I would not tell you my true feelings on society, for it would be more than your innocent ears could bear. But rest assured, my dear, there is no one whose affections I would prefer to have than yours, no home I would rather be in than the one we build, between us." He nodded towards her family. "No family I would rather have for my own than yours."

"I see." Amelia's eyes shone with amusement, but there was a shadow of worry in her next words. "You marry me for my family, then."

Ben did not answer straight away, and she feared, for a moment, that he had taken her words too seriously. Worse, there was some truth to them.

"I marry you for *you*," he said, quietly. "Recall, when first we met I had no notion who you were, but that you knew my sister and thought none-too-highly of me."

"But you did not love me then!" Amelia protested. "You shall not rewrite history to suggest you did."

"I shall not rewrite history," Ben agreed, with a pained smile. "I have been too often on the receiving end of history rewritten. But I will say I was intrigued by you. You were so unlike any young woman I had met before - yes I speak of the ladies I met *in society* before you ask again why I could not stand to be a part of it. Not a single young lady of the *ton* compares even a fraction to my dear Amelia, and how strange it feels to say those words aloud when I have thought them to myself so often these past weeks."

"Strange?" Amelia glanced at him.

"Wonderful." Ben smiled, sneaking close enough to drop a kiss on her cheek when he could be sure of their not being observed. "I can scarcely believe that you choose to hear them, though, and not seek to be away from me. Can you really care to marry such a man as me? Although the worst of the rumours swirling around me is false, I cannot claim to have led a completely blameless life." He swallowed, and it seemed to Amelia as if the words that came next were painful and difficult for him to say, but say them he did. "I teased you about my being like a villain from one of your books, but I suppose it is not so far from the truth."

He looked so anxious for a moment that Amelia was surprised. Where was the confident Devereaux who always had an answer and whose teasing usually served only to make *her* squirm? She laced her fingers through his.

"You are no literary villain," she said, confidently. When he looked at her, she smiled. "You are real, and whatever has or has not happened, in my past or yours, is done. What matters now is the present and the future. I think we stand a chance of having a happy one, but that depends as much on me as it does on you. We must work together to make it what we want it to be, and that will be adventure enough for me."

"And me," Ben said, stopping walking altogether and pulling her into the first of many warm embraces.

Epilogue

Sir Benjamin Devereaux had attended more assemblies than he could count, but he could not remember ever having looked forward to one more. He had anticipated the evening being something to be endured, rather than enjoyed, his stepmother had seen to that. Instead, he was welcomed back into the heart of the town that had once shunned him, although he could not take credit for the change. He knew his reputation had been cleared not by his own merits but by the actions of his friends. Admiral Sudbury was popular in the Westham, and he had ensured people knew the truth about his new friend, particularly when rumours began to circulate about Devereaux making an offer for the admiral's daughter. People still whispered but the eyes that fixed on the young Sir Benjamin were more likely tinged with curiosity and interest than suspicion. He was handsome, and what's more, he was happy and with the charming Amelia on his arm no matriarch could stay long opposed to him.

"I hope, Amelia, that you will be content to dance the first dance with me," he remarked, as the crowds began to take their places for the first dance. "I do not wish to deprive these other gentlemen of inviting you to dance..." He glanced around the room, his eyes roaming with satisfaction over the figure of Mr Connelly, who looked undeniably mournful as he saw the prize he had once thought his on the arm of another. "No, we have promised always to be honest with one another." He grinned. "I am *delighted* to deprive every other gentleman the pleasure of dancing with you."

"*Every* gentleman?"

Ben's words had carried as far as Arthur's ears, and Amelia's brother frowned.

"I hope you do not think I will surrender every claim on my sister, simply because she is to be your wife." He peered around at Amelia. "Milly, we shall dance the jig, just as we did as children. You shan't claim to be too grown up to dance with your brother after so many years apart."

Amelia's smile grew as she saw more than one pair of feminine eyes seek out the much-discussed Captain Sudbury.

"I am sure I do not wish to disappoint any other young *ladies* by taking their place on your arm, Arthur..."

He hooted and turned towards a pretty young lady with auburn hair who had caught his eye.

"I see now, Amelia, why you are so fond of these gatherings," Ben remarked. "For you are surrounded by your friends as well as your family."

"I am sure to you it is quite provincial," she said, moving closer to him as the music began. "How can it possibly compare with the dances you attended in London, surrounded by scandal and filled to the brim with fashionable, elegant people?"

Ben's eyes traversed the noisy, crowded assembly room, shabby despite its festive decorations, and he smiled. He tightened his grip on the young lady who, in a few short weeks, would be his wife, and felt more at home in himself, in his life, than he had ever thought possible.

"I can scarcely tell you how well it compares, Milly, dear," he whispered, using the name that was reserved only for her closest friends and family, and which still seemed so precious to him that he dared not use it more than on the rarest of occasions when he felt most aware of the prize he held. "To dance, here, surrounded by friends and with my soon-to-be bride on my arm, I cannot imagine a single place on earth I would rather be."

Amelia's eyes met his as the first notes of the piece began and for a moment it was as if the whole world melted away, leaving none but the two of them.

"Nor I," Amelia said, as they took the first steps of their first dance, together.

The End

About the Author

Meg Osborne[2] is an avid reader, tea drinker and unrepentant history nerd. She writes sweet historical romance stories and Jane Austen fanfiction, and can usually be found knitting, dreaming up new stories, or on twitter @megoswrites[3]

For updates and new release news – and for a free book! – sign up to Meg's newsletter list here[4]

---

1. https://megosbornewrites.com/

2. https://megosbornewrites.com/

3. https://twitter.com/megoswrites

4. https://dl.bookfunnel.com/1q3ks9bpku

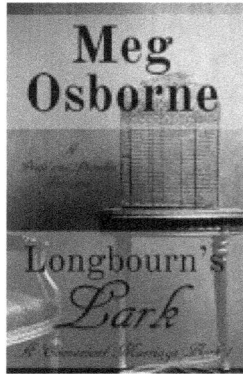

About the Author

Meg Osborne is an avid reader, tea drinker and unrepentant history nerd. She writes sweet historical romance stories and Jane Austen fanfiction, and can usually be found knitting, dreaming up new stories, or on twitter @megoswrites

Read more at www.megosbornewrites.com.

Lightning Source UK Ltd.
Milton Keynes UK
UKHW011006180123
415553UK00001B/237